RESURRECTION HALL
A Mansion World Odyssey
by Richard E. Warren

THE SEVEN MANSION WORLDS

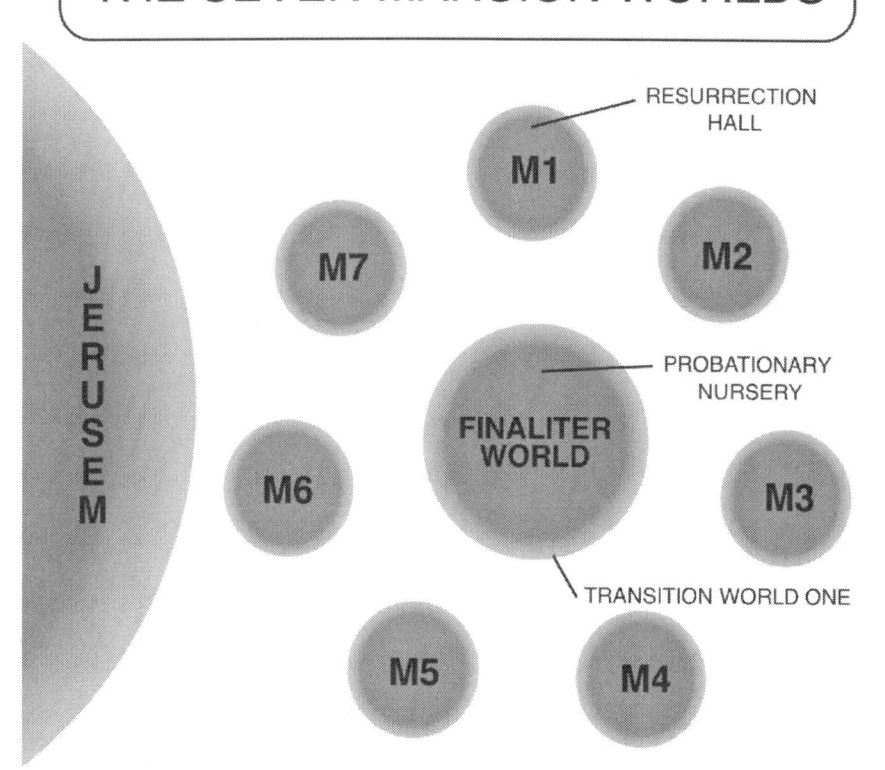

- M1 — RESURRECTION HALL
- M2
- M3
- M4 — TRANSITION WORLD ONE
- M5
- M6
- M7
- FINALITER WORLD — PROBATIONARY NURSERY
- JERUSEM

RESURRECTION HALL – A MANSION WORLD ODYSSEY

RESURRECTION HALL – A MANSION WORLD ODYSSEY

"In my Father's house are many mansions."
(341.7) 30:4.17

ABOUT THE AUTHOR

Richard "Rick" Warren is a father, grandfather, retired repairman, veteran, and thirty-year student of *The Urantia Book*. He is a newly published fiction writer living in Fort Worth, Texas, USA. "The Resurrection Hall" story was inspired by revelations in *The Urantia Book*, and created wholly by combining divine revelation with human imagination. It is the author's wish to provide a new vision of our next life, and to make life on Earth richer in knowledge and security of persistence of eternal meanings and spiritual values, alongside the survival of our loving personal relationships with God and the myriad children of time and space.

Edited by Rick Lyon
Cover design by Susan Lyon
Email: CosmicCreations606@gmail.com

This work uses quotations from the English-language translation of *The Urantia Book* published by Urantia Foundation, © Urantia Foundation, 533 W. Diversey Parkway, Chicago, Illinois 60614 USA +1 (773) 525-3319; http://www.urantia.org; all rights reserved. The views expressed in this work are those of the author and do not necessarily represent the views of Urantia Foundation or its affiliates.

All rights reserved. This book or any portion thereof may not be reproduced or used in any manner whatsoever without the express written permission of the publisher except for the use of brief quotations in a book review. Printed in the United States of America.

ISBN-13: 978-1-5455866-6-2
ISBN-10: 1-5455866-6-7
Copyright © 2017 by Richard E. Warren
www.resurrectionhall.com

RESURRECTION HALL – A MANSION WORLD ODYSSEY

"Throughout all eternity you will recall the profound memory impressions of your first witnessing of these resurrection mornings."
(533.3) 47:3.5

RESURRECTION HALL – A MANSION WORLD ODYSSEY

PREFACE

Eighty-three verbatim quotes from *The Urantia Book* were used in the writing of this book. Each paragraph containing a quote has the number of the Paper, Section, and Paragraph. *The Urantia Book's* text is available for reading and downloading in the major languages at urantia.org. Urantia Foundation was established to preserve and disseminate this unique revelatory text. The English version of *The Urantia Book* is not copyrighted; therefore can its text be used, preferably with attribution to its source, without limit.

The words Urantia and Urantian were also used in the writing of Resurrection Hall. Both words are trademarked by Urantia Foundation. The uses of these trademarked words in this story complies with Urantia Foundation's 'fair use policy.'

This story was created using imagination and revelation. Without the revelations of the Urantia Papers, no such story could be possible. All credit for it must go to the Revelators who furnished the text of the greatest book ever conceived, written and published; and to God who created imagination, and who even indwells us.

RESURRECTION HALL – A MANSION WORLD ODYSSEY

RESURRECTION HALL – A MANSION WORLD ODYSSEY

Dedicated to:
Erin, Joannie, and Rachelle

RESURRECTION HALL – A MANSION WORLD ODYSSEY

RESURRECTION HALL – A MANSION WORLD ODYSSEY

TABLE OF CONTENTS

CHAPTER:	TITLE	PAGE
1	Awakening	1
2	Reunion	8
3	First Worship, First Night	16
4	First Morning, Call to Service	25
5	Banquet Hall Reception	34
6	Andon and Fonta's Welcome	42
7	Sixth and Seventh Course	50
8	Orientation	58
9	Meeting Solonia and First Flight	69
10	Passenger Birds and The Registry	78
11	Dinner And A Concert	85
12	Religious Experience, The Evangels	95
13	Touring M1	104
14	Seraphic Transport, Arriving on M2	112
15	Family Visits, Jesus' Life Presentation	121
16	Touring M3, First Visit To Jerusem	131
17	Adamic Estate, Broadcast Center	141
18	Touring M5, T5, M6, T6 And M7	149
19	Father's and Prison Worlds, Call to Fuse	160
20	Fusion, New Beginning	171
	Index of Urantia Book Quotes	177

RESURRECTION HALL – A MANSION WORLD ODYSSEY

RESURRECTION HALL – A MANSION WORLD ODYSSEY

~ Chapter 1 ~
Awakening

Her eyes popped open. She drew her first breath, then another, deeper one. She was standing and having to focus on balance. Two beings were there to steady her, one on the left and one on the right. She somehow knew they could be none other than her Guardian Angels. Suddenly her mind was flooded with images. Her faithful and beloved Adjuster arrived with the transcripts of her personal memories of life on Urantia. She hadn't yet grasped that this is Resurrection Hall on Mansion One, but she did realize and *know* she was alive again.

This new unification of body, mind, soul, personality and Adjuster was an intense event of wonder and awe, also one of rapid adjustment. Next, the two angels came directly in front of her. They moved in very close; she felt embraced like never before. She then realized she was standing on a mansion world and this was her first post-mortal encounter, that her soul must be there also, and that her identity was indeed reconstituted and intact. She was resurrected!

Simultaneously with that embrace she strongly sensed the presence of her indwelling Thought Adjuster, her Paradise Partner. Adjuster memories of Earth life were flooding her mind, as fast as she could assimilate them. As the moments passed, the eternal significance of this event was coming together in her mind, her new mind. How pristine and vast that mind seemed at this moment. In all eternity she would never forget this day of awakening. She had indeed survived and was now breathing and living on another world. How wonderful, how great, how fulfilling!!

Along with her Guardian Angels there were several other beings gathered around who seemed vaguely familiar. Some she must have known on Urantia, some not. She felt so very warm, energized, confident and fearless, but needed time to adjust. It was overwhelming, so many pictures were flashing in her mind. It was a story. Her story! Past events were quickly connecting this new mind to her life on Urantia. She was remembering and reassembling experiences in greater detail and establishing their chronological order.

Her beloved family, where were they? She thought to ask, but the words didn't come out. The angels seemed to be mumbling at her. What were they saying? It wasn't making sense because she was not yet completely connected. And too, she was feeling overwhelmed by the intense beauty and palpable friendliness of the beings and environment to which she had just awoken. Her mind was foggy for an instant, then clear, then foggy again. Clarity began to dominate, and her spirit began to soar on the growing realization of resurrection.

After a moment more her focus and attention stabilized and shifted to the immediate surroundings, primarily the astonishingly beautiful and caring beings attending her. Their faces were so lovely and well defined. And they were somehow helping her awaken a multitude of memories. So many were coming at once.

At the same time, her soul was flying ever higher at the realization of the vindication of her faith in God and Michael, her belief in continuing life, and the validity of the revelations she was now beginning to recall, about resurrection on Mansonia. With every moment's passing she was more fully aware she was a soul survivor, an Agondonter from Urantia, newly awakened on Mansonia.

All she could think at that moment was, 'thank you God, thank you Michael, thank you Mother!!!'

Again, she attempted to speak, wanting to say, 'breathing is incredible!' With each breath she could feel powerful energy coursing through her marvelous, strong, pain-free, highly sensitive, nascent body. The smell of the air was truly rich. She thought but couldn't say: 'what a lovely aroma here.'

Looking around she noticed everything and everyone was beautifully clean, sparkling and intricately appointed. The floor and low walls were made of lustrous metals and lined with inlaid jewels and gems vastly diverse in hue and form.

Every being in sight was aglow with an unmistakable and warm luminescence. The sky was a magnificent cloudless vault of deep blue, without a shining sun, a moon, or a cloud.

As she gazed over the resurrection scene, too amazed to speak, the angel on her left put before her what appeared to be a three dimensional mirror. She watched closely as the image rotated, then in complete amazement thought, 'O my God! That IS me?!' She knew it had to be her, but what a change. This body is young, smooth, and straight; vision and hearing are superb. Next she took note of her hands and feet, wiggling her fingers and toes, they are perfectly formed and very sensitive.

On her body was a light wrap, a truly beautiful super-shimmering fabric — a sort of morontia material she thought, material that automatically form-fits to each body. Morontia! She always enjoyed contemplating that word. And now she felt much like a super version of her old self, one she had often imagined. She touched the image and uttered, "This is me, morontia me, I am alive, I AM alive!"

Everyone standing around said in unison, "You are!" She could communicate, she could hear and be heard, and in a language she understood! All was coming together now; greater and greater perspective was accumulating with each passing moment. She was awake and alive in the Resurrection Hall of Mansion World Number One. But where was her family? Why were they not here to greet her? Had her grandparents, parents, dead cousins and friends not survived? Many questions were now surfacing in her nimble new mind.

"Where is my husband? Is Saro here?"

"Come with us, Kala," her right side Guardian said.

She felt compelled to confirm who they were: "You are my Guardian Angels, aren't you?"

"Yes," they replied together. Her angels were so very beautiful and charming, she felt an instant affection and familiarity with them. How strange and wonderful to actually see and hear her angels, even though she had often felt their presence on Urantia.

But who were the other brilliant and shining beings around her? Should she introduce herself? Evidently introductions were to come later. Kala realized each of these beings must be important to her, but couldn't quite place them. At this point, only her Guardians and her Paradise Partner felt familiar. It was dawning on her how much there was to learn, and recall.

She attempted to move and almost fell forward. Both angels caught her by the arms steadying her.

"Give me a second," she said, then consciously put one foot forward, then the other. She was walking for the first time. It wasn't hard, just new. Everything and everyone here somehow felt greatly amplified and improved, but the adjustment was not instantaneous. Certain of her memories and skills were returning with each moment. But she had the distinct feeling there were many other memories, ones she could not yet access.

Movement, sight, hearing, smell, touch, the ability to experience and comprehend — all these were present as on Urantia, but here they are magnified and sharpened. She hadn't gained or lost anything, except this new and amazing body-mind, along with, of course, the priceless gift of soul and personality survival. This was her first step toward eternal union with the Indweller from Paradise, fusion with her Adjuster.

For the first time she glanced at the horizon and everything and everyone in between. There were other groups of beings — much like the one she was in — everywhere, many thousands of them. As far as she could see there were similar groupings.

She took more steps as the angels gently guided her to the adjacent resurrection chamber. At its center was a being she recognized immediately. Kala and Saro locked eyes for the first time as resurrected beings. She rushed to him, he lunged toward her, as their angels and other beings in attendance converged around them.

It was a moment for the ages, a memory they would never, ever forget, wherein a one-time husband and wife meet on Mansonia, and in morontia form, for their first embrace after 55 years of life together as human mortals on Urantia. Evidently they had passed the great test of mortal incarnation and embryonic soul development.

Saro's first steps were attempted when he saw her approaching. He almost fell too, in the move toward his longtime mate and friend, except for the aid of his attending Guardians. Kala and Saro's first embrace was one of transcendent love, too beautiful and fulfilling for words. Suddenly they both felt tremendous gratitude for the God who made this resurrection and reunification possible. Great tears came to their new eyes, tears of appreciation and joy. What a marvelous plan our Father has created for time and space ascenders. And to think, what they are seeing and experiencing during these first moments of life as resurrected beings are but the barest beginnings of morontia life.

Kala and Saro's reconnection brought up many, many questions for which they had few answers. But they were having more and more memory flashes of life on Urantia, experiences that had significant meaning and value, moments of genuine religious experience, things of great spiritual import, and well-established relationships with their families, friends, and former teammates.

Obviously they had retained language, sensory, and movement abilities. But most prominent in their minds at this moment was the series of spiritual connections that brought them to this astonishing place, and in a new body. Kala was recalling the time when Michael's spirit touched her, after which she took an abiding interest in the revelations and teachings of *The Urantia Book*. Saro was recalling receiving God's reply after he prayed, asking if he should marry Kala, and receiving a resounding 'YES.' But how and when did they die? So many questions needed to be answered.

At that point their Guardians introduced themselves. Kala and Saro thanked them sincerely and profusely for the safekeeping of their souls, and for all they did pre-death, much of which they were only now realizing. Always had Kala felt the Guardians' guidance and the Adjuster's influence. Saro did in a measure also sense and appreciate their work for his spiritual well-being and physical safety when he and Kala were on Urantia.

Their four angels drew near and all six embraced in a charming little huddle. How warm and full of love Kala and Saro felt. For decades the Guardians had worked with the pair, unseen, helping them spread the teachings and the text of *The Urantia Book*. And now their trusted Guardian Angels were visible, even embraceable. Meeting them face-to-face was a rewarding and confirmatory experience. At the same time, the feeling of affirmation of their long-held faith in the existence of God and his angels was immensely gratifying, satisfying, even thrilling.

Suddenly, and simultaneously, Saro and Kala recalled dying. Being together again somehow sparked this traumatic memory. They drew a deep breath, looked into each others' beautiful new eyes, and recalled that it was a quick and merciful death. They were flying a single engine airplane — both were pilots — delivering Urantia Books to a new library system on a large but remote island in western Indonesia. On board was one box of each translation, as requested by the chief librarian.

A storm cloud was behind them, so they felt safe. But when they flew over a high ridge they were confronted with another and bigger cloud. There was no choice except to go on, but it was not to be. Lightening was all around. They thought of going higher, over the storm, or quickly landing somewhere. Before they could act, a tremendous bolt struck the plane instantly destroying it, along with the mortal bodies of Kala and Saro Maylon.

Amazingly, all of the books were later found, largely intact, and still wrapped in plastic. And all did eventually reach their destination.

"When did we die?" Saro asked his Guardians.

"Three days ago," they replied together. Saro and Kala were both thinking what charming voices the angels have.

"We qualified for the three day express!" Saro exclaimed, "Just like we were hoping for." They smiled, embraced, and kissed. It was difficult not to smile, given their happy new situation.

And they both couldn't help noticing how youthful and vibrant their morontia bodies are. And every second memories of Urantia, their former estate, were emerging in their beautiful, new, morontia minds.

~ Chapter 2 ~
Reunion

Next, a Pilgrim Receiver stepped up, introducing herself by name and title, and addressing the pair by their first names. The Receiver sincerely and touchingly welcomed Kala and Saro to Mansion One, to their "new lives as semi-physical beings," and to "their first stop on the way to Paradise." At that moment they were feeling more like super-beings.

Just then Kala recalled that Pilgrim Receivers are a type of Morontia Companion who are created by Michael's mate, the Divine Minister of Nebadon. Before they died, they both had near encyclopedic knowledge of *The Urantia Book's* text. Those recollections were quickly falling into place. Gradually but certainly, reflections of their former lives were coalescing in their morontia minds, thanks to Adjuster memory transcripts, acquired soul values, and God-given personality, now combined and resurrected in a new morontia form.

After their introduction and welcoming, the Receiver expressed genuine pleasure at meeting these two Agondonters from Urantia, whose life records she had reviewed prior to this meeting. Kala and Saro couldn't help but notice how charming and genial she was.

The Receiver then signaled two in their reception group to come forward. "Kala, meet your parents." She was completely stunned at first, then very happy. Of course! How could she not recognize them? The difficulty was that everyone appeared young, vibrant, unbent, and unwrinkled.

She reached out and took one parent in each arm for an affectionate embrace, then looked into their lovely morontian eyes. Such a thrilling experience to be alive and in another body that is so exquisitely sensitive and highly responsive. But to accept and integrate the fact that her elderly parents are also now in new, robust, healthy bodies would take time. It then occurred to Kala that everyone here is more sibling-like than an elder or a junior, that generational differences disappear when everyone is forever young.

Now she was once again with her dear mother and father. She had often wondered who would be there to greet her at resurrection. She exchanged words of endearment with her parents, and laid plans "to catch up." Then Saro embraced his parents-in-law, suddenly recalling the many study group meetings he and Kala attended at their home on Urantia. Kala was a second-generation reader, Saro was a first, having learned of the book from Kala.

Then suddenly, Kala recognized two others. Her maternal grandparents, kindly relatives she truly cherished when on Urantia. She embraced them heartily, and at the same time came to a fuller realization that she must now begin relating to her parents and grandparents as equals, as ascending peers and aspiring souls, contemporaries in the long pursuit of perfection. Her grandparents congratulated them on survival, and secured a promise from the pair for a long visit.

"And you may recall this person." The Receiver beckoned one that was, without a doubt, her cousin, for whom Kala had cried and grieved much when cancer took her away during late adolescence. They were more like sisters and best friends than cousins.

"Hello Kala!"

"Joy, you're here!" They hugged and danced in a small circle. What good news that she too had survived, and now they had eternity ahead, which no disease could prevent. Kala looked up to her, deeply admiring the courage, wisdom, and faith Joy displayed during the illness and right up to her death. They conferred for a moment, planning to meet later for a "day on the town."

All of Kala's family members then circled and embraced her. She quickly looked each one in the eye, then kissed their cheek. Saro was beaming at the beauty of this reunion. He watched with true joy and anticipation, knowing the others in their group, the ones standing back watching this resurrection scene, might be his relations. But he couldn't yet identify any.

The Receiver then asked, "Saro, do you recognize this person?" He peered into the being's face. Suddenly it hit him.

"Will! You're here too! I'm so glad."

Will died in war when Saro was only nineteen. He was all but crushed by his brother's death. It was a difficult and soul-searching period in his life. Saro had always admired and emulated his only sibling. Will was much older than Saro, and truly a good person. The two of them hugged and agreed to meet, talk, and roam, after they were settled.

Next, two male cousins came face to face with Saro. The three of them had been best of friends all their Urantian lives. Both cousins had preceded Saro in death, and he missed them greatly. Always was it a memorable occasion when, as boys, and as men, they gathered to make music, oftentimes with Will as bandleader.

They shook hands and shared a warm, fraternal embrace. Saro couldn't have been happier, except he wondered why his parents and grandparents were not there to welcome him, as were Kala's. He thought to ask his cousins if their parents had survived, for he loved them too. They informed Saro that his aunt and uncle were expected to reappear at the next millennial resurrection.

Saro hesitated to ask where his parents were. He well remembered they showed little interest in things spiritual, and worried he might not see them again. But he was already feeling trust and affinity for these morontia beings, realizing that all questions would find answers in good time.

Sensing his question, Will informed Saro, "mom and dad are still asleep." He was disappointed but happy to know they would be resurrected at some point. Saro was now recalling the teachings about resurrection; some fuse with their Indweller while on the planet of nativity; some die and are re-personalized after three days as he and Kala had; and some become sleeping survivors who will awake in morontia bodies at millennial or dispensational resurrections.

After the introductions and welcoming, the group was quiet for a brief moment, enjoying the aftermath of this seemingly miraculous resurrection, one that was a routine occurrence for the Receiver. Then, spontaneously, the two families and their newly resurrected relatives began socializing, introducing one another, and discussing others they knew of, ones who were or were not yet resurrected. Kala and Saro laughed for the first time during the exchange. How good it was to laugh and feel the joy of being, how rich everything and everyone here! This went on for a while. The Receiver appeared to encourage the social interaction. Obviously it had a stabilizing and bonding effect on her newborn charges.

Right now, consciousness of survival was uppermost in their quick and powerful new minds, along with an appreciation for this warm reception by their beloved family members and Guardians, so charmingly facilitated by the Receiver. They could sense that much thought, time, and energy had gone into planning and arranging this birthing, this new beginning for two lowly but ascending pilgrims from Urantia. All the while, the pair was becoming more aware of the hive of activity around them, as tens of thousands of simultaneous resurrections unfolded in the great hall.

Next, the Receiver asked for the group's attention. She pointed to the center of Resurrection Hall saying they should begin moving in that direction. The vast circular hall is divided into seven enormous sections that very gradually slope toward the center. Each of the seven sections is dedicated to the resurrection of one of the races that typify life on evolutionary worlds. Around the seven sections is an outer ring where beings who belonged to no one race are resurrected.

Kala and Saro were both of mixed race inheritance on Urantia. Their mothers were long time friends who had immigrated to the United States from Indonesia with a small group of World War II refugees. After the war, they met, dated, and married American men — newly discharged soldiers. Kala had two brothers, Saro and Will had no other siblings.

The pair grew up not far from each other in a peaceful suburb of Chicago, but had only passing contact until they entered the same college. It was there Kala introduced Saro to *The Urantia Book*. Kala's father was led to the revelation by a friend at work who invited him to one of the Sunday afternoon 'Forum' sessions held at the Sadler's north side residence during the late 1930's and early '40's.

Kala's dad attended the Forum for several years before going off to war. After the war, he met and married Kala's mother. When he heard *The Urantia Book* was published in 1955, he bought a copy. He and Kala's mother became life long students. And they were very pleased when their daughter embraced its teachings, but only after a somewhat troubled adolescence.

Kala and Saro had three children while on Urantia, and they were grandparents of five, with two more on the way when they so suddenly departed for Mansonia. They were both thinking of their families at this moment, anticipating the day they might all be reunited on Mansonia. And the wonderful surprises their children and grandchildren have in store!

Their group was quite a distance from the central temple, but it looked especially beautiful from their point of view, emitting a soft and appealing light. They could see a tall spire at its center, reaching into the sky, supported by seven thin beams, one extending from each section.

Saro asked, "Kala, remember the Temple of New Life described in *The Urantia Book*?"

"Yes, I do. That has to be it," she replied.

Their Receiver said, "Newborn pilgrims inevitably wish to thank the Archangels and Life Carriers who helped with their resurrection, but even more they desire to offer worshipful thanksgiving to the Paradise Father for making survival and endless life possible."

"I do feel that need," said Kala. Saro nodded agreement.

Slowly, their group began walking toward the hall's center. These two Agondonters from Urantia were feeling very much in the moment, drinking in one wonder after another. They were having joyful thoughts, imagining living, working, playing, resting, and worshiping amid such wonders all the time, everywhere. Evidently their relatives who welcomed them had become accustomed to this wealthy environment, free of animal fear, cosmic ignorance, and physical disease. Their families were thoroughly enjoying watching Kala and Saro's reactions to the newness and thrill of being alive in a fresh body with a new mind, and on a better world.

"This hall can facilitate a million resurrections at once, as I recall," said Saro.

"That is correct," replied the Receiver. "Yours is a special resurrection, and a relatively small one. Approximately 200,000."

Now all the groups were breaking up and moving toward the hall's center, ambling down the broad aisles between each of the seven sections. What a joyous occasion, what a glorious place! They were both thinking that the experience of this moment is worth any suffering one may have encountered in the first life as a corporeal being. Words failed them while this reality filled them to the brim with the sheer joy of the consciousness of resurrection on a mansion world.

As their group moved down the aisle toward the central Temple along with the gathering flow, Kala and Saro observed the faces and forms of other newborns, comparing them to each other, to their relatives, and to the Morontia Companions, all the while delighting in the underlying premise of Mansonia; the idea and ideal of cosmic unity — everyone knowing and venerating the same God.

No longer were they in a world where people are forever

arguing over religious ideology, struggling for secular power and influence, and fighting over territorial sovereignty. There is a palpable fearlessness and a pervasive spiritual unity on Mansonia that the pair liked very much. It felt like they had come home to a place they had never been.

The closer to the Temple they came, the better they could discern its main features: bowl-shaped with a slightly elevated rim, and gigantic to Saro's and Kala's wide eyes. The great hall of resurrection and its central temple are completely open to the bright sunless sky. No rain, no lightening, no earthquakes, and no hurricanes trouble this sphere.

The Receiver pointed to a majestic sculpture at the very center of the temple and said, "That is the Michael Memorial. It has Gabriel's seal, with the words: *'In commemoration of the mortal transit of Jesus of Nazareth on Urantia.'* " (188:3.11) Saro and Kala were once again following in his footsteps.

They were noticing that beautifully intricate artwork covered every surface, that well appointed sculpture accentuated every corner and post, with which morontia plant life was very tastefully integrated. Lovely purplish-violet leaved vines with an array of colored flowers were climbing each side of the shiny arched entrance to the Temple of New Life. Indeed, the temple area itself is magnificently embellished with sparkling gems, shimmering metals, and shining jewels from its outer rim to the intervening concentric seating arrangement, to the round stage at its center and lowest point.

One of Kala's Guardians said to the pair, "We leave you in the Receiver's experienced hands for the moment, and go to officially register your resurrection and record your status as morontia survivors. We will rejoin you after your commune. And know that we are always watching over you, even if not seen."

The pair thanked them, embraced them, and took note of their quickly growing affection for them. The four Guardians then moved away so quickly as to vanish.

The Receiver led them through the arches and down to

their reserved seats. The chairs were very comfortable, with high backs and cushioned armrests. They were made from materials that seemed to embrace and comfort their morontia skin. Sitting for the first time, Saro and Kala looked at each other and wondered silently and simultaneously what the rest of Mansonia could be like, given the astonishing things they had so far witnessed.

The din of thousands chattering filled their new ears. Hearing was astonishingly clear and easily focused. Indeed, all their senses were becoming sharper. As the other resurrectees entered the temple and sought out their places, Saro and Kala sat watching, listening, and waiting. They were thoroughly enjoying the spikes and nuances of their new senses, stimulated by the sights and sounds of 200,000 fellow resurrectees during these initial moments as morontians.

It took awhile for all groups to enter and find their seats. As they did, Kala and Saro sat side by side, continuing to gaze at this fantastic scene of their fellow beings, all gathering in this one place to give thanks to, and engage in the worship of, the God of All Creation. These humble pilgrims have come together here at this time and place for a celebration of life everlasting, and the One who made it possible, beginning anew this very day for two God-loving Agondonters from Urantia.

~ Chapter 3 ~
First Worship, First Night

When all were inside and seated, an astonishingly beautiful angel — a "Conductor of Worship," whispered their Receiver — entered the central stage and lifted her hands high, arresting and focusing attention. The audience fell silent. The Conductor remained still with hands held high. Then, as if from everywhere, there came a most wondrous sound. Then began another one even more appealing. Music! They were hearing morontia music. How rich, how moving! They sat in rapt attention as the sounds intermingled and harmonized. It was truly celestial in tone and composure. The sounds made them better realize the range and acuity of their hearing.

Spontaneously, everyone genuflected. Some took to their knees, some simply sat and bowed their heads. It was so natural and so appropriate at a time like this. These two Agondonters were feeling immensely thankful for continuing life. The Receivers were ever grateful to be midwives to more new souls for God whom they too adored; their dedication and love for this service was obvious. Kala's and Saro's relatives were enjoying this almost as much as they were, now fondly recalling their first experiences giving thanks and worshiping as morontia beings.

Kala praised God, silently, in her thoughts. Saro too. In fact all the resurrectees were doing just that. The music was rousing everyone to greater heights of emotional focus and thanksgiving. Tears began to flow from thousands of eyes. How can God create such things, and in such abundance? This prayerful interlude was deeply humbling and sublimely divine, perfect for this day of life-refreshing and resurrection on one of God's 'many mansions.'

Evidently, no words were going to be said. Music was the

language that transcended all idiomatic barriers during this experience. Then it stopped. A collective moan of pleasure and joy swept over the gathering. Then the music began again, but this was much different. These sounds soothed and quieted their minds. They all then felt a strong urge to worship, to internally embrace their indwelling Adjusters who had so patiently and persistently worked within that they could be here, on high, living, breathing, and worshiping a great God, a perfect Father, as newborn morontians who will never again die.

It was difficult to judge how long this worship session went on. Saro and Kala were so caught up that time seemed to disappear, and God never felt nearer. They also expressed, in their own minds in their own ways, heartfelt gratitude and loving affection for our creator father and mother, Michael, and the Divine Minister. It felt as if they were in their deepest embrace ever, with a trinity of divine lovers, the Universal Father, the Spirit of Truth, and the Holy Spirit.

The music gradually shaded off into silence as all remained perfectly still and content in worshipful unity and loving appreciation. At that moment, one of Kala's favorite lines in *The Urantia Book* about worship came to mind, one she had memorized and often repeated in times of stress, *"...the act of worship becomes increasingly all-encompassing until it eventually attains the glory of the highest experiential delight and the most exquisite pleasure known to created beings."* (27:7.1) And this was only their first taste of worship as resurrected beings. One they will remember forever.

The Conductor leading this marvelous gathering returned to center stage, not uttering a word, simply raising, then lowering her hands and bowing. That was their exit signal. Saro and Kala's Receiver leaned toward them saying: "Time to go to your lodging."

The throngs began filing out of this wonder evoking temple, each resurrection group reforming and moving toward the exit arches, each group being led by a Pilgrim Receiver to a different lodge in the Melchizedek sector. As they were exiting,

Saro and Will's two cousins regretfully excused themselves, leaving for a prior commitment and promising to reconnect with Saro and Kala when schedules permit. They warmly embraced and congratulated the pair, then departed.

As the group strolled toward the Melchizedek sector the Receiver said to them, "When you have been properly welcomed and oriented during the next two days, you will be free to explore and become familiar with the Mansonia training regime. First, you may wish to view the registry of those already here, your deceased relatives and friends. After the initial ten days of 'vacation', you will begin the Paradise journey anew. For now, enjoy, explore, and most of all, talk with others. Translators will always be available should they be required. And one or both of your personal angelic guardians is always near."

Both Saro and Kala then recalled that a day in Mansonia was almost three times as long as a day on Urantia. That meant they had about a month to explore, learn, observe, discover, connect and revel in this new life, this amazing mansion world.

Their four Guardian Angels reappeared at that moment. How interesting was the appearance of these Guardian Seraphim. They have heads, arms, and feet, but their friction shields were compactly set in their backs. The angels spread these so-called wings before they take flight in the cold depths of space, wrapping them around themselves and any cargo they may have, into the shape of a torpedo. The Guardians fairly glowed with an appealing luminescence. They were obviously extremely bright and capable. And they could move so quickly that they seemed to disappear.

One of Saro's angels said, "We four Guardians wish to convey our congratulations on your resurrection. For many decades we worked with and for you on Urantia always unseen and unheard. Now we are visible and you can hear these words: We love you and want to express our appreciation for your willing cooperation and wise choosing as humans on

Urantia. Not all angels are so fortunate to have such cooperative wards." Her words were so tender, kind, and sincere, the pair was moved to embrace them again.

"Thank you for watching over us all those years," Saro said. "Your faithful guidance must surely be part of the reason we are here now."

Kala added, "I'm very happy to finally see and speak with you face to face. I can recall thinking of you, trying to imagine your appearance." She then asked one of her Guardians, "Would you mind unfolding your shields? Can you? Is that permitted?" Without hesitation the four fanned out and slowly did so. The group stopped to watch Kala's and Saro's reaction on seeing angels with 'wings' spread for the first time.

Their jaws went slack and they ceased breathing as they witnessed each Guardian's double set of shields unfurl, extending from the seraphim's heads to their angelic toes. Angels were indeed charming and lovely creatures to behold.

"Your shields look as much like energy as living flesh," said Saro.

It was a great thrill for them to be able to see and interact with these amazing beings, these mind ministers and personal carriers, who will literally fly every ascending son and daughter of God to his Paradise home. The angels rejoiced that their beloved wards were successful, which meant they were successful and now open to the real possibility of journeying to Paradise also. The love among the four angels and their two subjects, which took origin on Urantia, was now quite obvious, they could all feel and enjoy it. After a short embrace the angels departed. But first they promised that one of them was, "always watching and available."

As the group approached the ascending pilgrim's residential area, the pair's eyes widened. They could not help noticing its charming architecture and artistic details. Nothing was left to chance in the flora either, no weeds were apparent. Their residence is an elegantly appointed area with plants of many varieties, dazzling flowers of colors they had to stop and examine, smell, and marvel over. There was a short, winding path to the entrance of their lodging.

"This is so beautiful," they said simultaneously, then laughed as they could not stop marveling at everything they had seen on this first day, during these first impressionable hours as newly resurrected beings. The group of relatives continued to watch the pair as they entered the roofless abode, vicariously enjoying their first day's experiences as mansion world progressors.

"I don't think I could ever have imagined the beauty and variety of morontia materials," commented Kala as she looked over their surroundings. Saro was now recalling something that always intrigued him, written by one who was granted a vision of Mansonia. The apostle Paul wrote, and was quoted in *The Urantia Book*, *"They have in heaven a better and more enduring substance."* (48:1.7) Then he remembered that morontia materials have one hundred more elements than the one hundred evolving planets have. And how well the morontians have used them, thought Saro.

The walls of their lodging were high enough for privacy, but the outer rooms had transparent spaces, mansion world windows. At the center of this magnificently constructed little building was a bedroom without windows. It was no less glorious in appearance than the other enclosures and edifices they had seen. The Receiver touched a panel and instantly the bedroom's walls became windows. "Have privacy if you like," she said. Touching the panel again, the artistically adorned walls returned. The bed was laced and layered in a most appealing fashion. The pair anticipated their first night's rest there, on this beautiful, peaceful world.

They then moved into the largest room. It had seating all around, with three tables and chairs in the center, obviously intended for guests and socializing. Appealing artwork embellished nearly every surface and article. Saro and Kala were all but over-awed at this point. To bring things into perspective and break any tension the pair might be feeling, Will asked his brother, "Hey Saro, how do you get to Paradise?"

"I don't know Will, how?" he said with a big smile, recalling his brother's quirky humorous side.

"PerFECT, perFECT, perFECT!" said Will with a broad smile and a wink.

They all chuckled. The relatives were recalling that was one of the first memes they learned on Mansonia. Saro and Kala were both classical musicians and, at that moment, realized Will's quip was a morontia twist on a trick question to aspiring musicians aiming for Urantia's highest recital hall — How do you get to Carnegie Hall? Practice, practice, practice!

Their Pilgrim Receiver asked them to sit while she spoke a few words of parting to the pair. "Enjoy the rest of the day dear Agondonters and new friends. Visit with your relatives, then spend your first night under Mansonia's stars. Please feel free to become familiar with the surrounding area, and to make yourselves comfortable here.

"Before they depart for the night, perhaps your friends will show you how to use the lodging's features and options." The group nodded. "Roam the sector if you like, I will be by for you tomorrow at dawn. I have a request to make of you two. But for now, relax. Tomorrow will be here soon enough."

They walked with the Receiver to the abode's entrance. She embraced the pair, after which they uttered their most profound appreciation. When the three reached the lodging's front gate, the Receiver gave them each a small, flat, round device, and said to make any request by simply asking the device. Finally, she assured them a Companion would be available all night adding, "and of course your Guardians are always only a thought away."

When they returned to the relatives inside their lovely lodging, now comfortably conversing with each other, Saro interrupted, holding up his device and asking, "Is this a 'harp of God?'"

Will stood and proclaimed loudly, "It's official Saro. You two are now morontia creatures!" Everyone applauded and Will proceeded to show them just a few of the rudimentary functions of this amazing but innocuous appearing device.

"Depict Jerusem's main temple," said Will to his harp.

Instantly a three dimensional image appeared before them. They froze and marveled at it as Will caused the image to rotate. All the sights and sounds coming from it were crystal sharp. "Show the main floor of the Jerusem communication center." The image changed to an astonishing array of visual displays, chart boards, and moving images.

"Is that a recording?" Saro asked.

"No. It's that easy to watch a live view of events and beings on another world," Will told them. The pair was shown other astonishing sights until they could watch no more. It was too overwhelming, so many beings of differing hues and morontia forms to fill their minds, plus endless architecture of breath-taking, artistic excellence. Will showed them one more place, the central temple on Mansion Two. They watched as temple goers moved about the remarkably intricate, be-gemmed and bejeweled structure. It fairly glowed with light they were certain no human eye could discern.

"Have you been there, in person?" asked Kala. "We have, and went there often," said her grandmother, "before we advanced to Mansion Three."

Her grandfather added, "Kala, what you will see between here and Jerusem will push back every imaginable limit you have of the possibilities of creative expression. Enjoy each and every minute to the utmost. You both will easily fit in here. It's so good to see you again, and to speak English again! It's been awhile. We almost didn't make it in time for your resurrection, so sudden was your graduation off Urantia."

"Sudden as a bolt of lightening," joked Will.

"Where do you live, mom and dad?" Kala asked.

"Mansion Two," they answered together. "So GOOD to have you here, Kala, Saro," said her mother. "Both your brothers are still sleeping, Kala."

"I was wondering," replied Kala. "And you Joy?"

"Also Mansion Two. You are going to love life here, it was made for ones like you."

"Mansion Two is my cloud also," said Will.

The day was long but they didn't tire of chatting, reminiscing, and laughing, especially when piecing together family stories of lessons learned from easy and hard times on Urantia. More and more memories of their former life were coalescing in their morontia minds as the conversations shifted back and forth, from that life to this one. Of course Saro and Kala asked many questions about Mansonia life, but not nearly enough. There was so very much to learn, do and see. On they communed until the sky became dusky, and the first stars of an unfamiliar night sky were seen through the pair's new eyes.

Kala's father walked over to a service counter, touched a small panel twice, and out came a tray of beautiful golden goblets filled with liquid. "Time to toast our new arrivals," he declared, and passed the tray around. They both were still having trouble adjusting to how young everyone appeared. But it did seem to lessen any distance between the generations.

Holding up his goblet, her father said in a most charming manner, "Kala and Saro, welcome to Mansonia."

"Welcome!" they all said in excellent harmony.

"What is it?" Kala asked her father.

"Time for your first taste of mansion world water, daughter."

They were all waiting and watching. Kala remarked, "Funny, we hadn't thought of drink or food until now." She and Saro looked at one another and made a lovely resonate sound by clinking their goblets together. Everyone held them high, then took a sip.

"That is *tasty*," said Saro, "it's very pure, isn't it?" Kala took another drink, a big one. Saro followed suit. Then they both drank it all to the cheers of the group. It was very satisfying. They asked for another, then a third cup. If water tastes this good to their morontia palate, how good will mansion world food taste? But they were feeling no hunger at this point, none at all.

The Pilgrim Receiver had arranged for their relatives to stay at an adjacent lodging, in order that Saro and Kala could be alone that night. When it was time to leave, each one congratulated the pair face to face. They exchanged words of familial love, and feelings of genuine joy over this mansion world reunion.

Kala and Saro fondly embraced each one before departing. The oneness of their spirits with these charming people became imprinted deeply on the pair. For a moment Kala contemplated the stupendous possibilities and limitless potentials for personal contact with a whole universe of friendly beings across eternity.

~ Chapter 4 ~
First Morning, Call to Service

After bidding their guests good night at the front gate, Saro and Kala turned and walked toward their new residence. They moved quietly, arm in arm, stopping, observing and simply breathing the magnificent air. Their new bodies were exquisitely healthy, and marvelously sensitive, surprisingly strong and responsive. They certainly weren't tired or needing rest.

Looking up at the moonless sky, with faint light from several nearby suns, evoked a kind of joy they hadn't felt before. They kissed under those stars for the first time.

"Well, seems we are no longer married," said Saro.

"I was wondering about that, and if we will ever be separated?"

They entered the cottage, turned off the interior lighting, and lay down for the first time. On their backs, staring up at the stars from their ample and divinely comfortable bed, Kala wondered aloud, "What direction is Paradise?"

"What do you think happens to the water we drank?" asked Saro. They laughed at the vast difference between their questions.

"These bodies are amazing, aren't they! Maybe water is evaporated through our morontia skin." Kala pinched Saro's left arm, "take off your wrap." she said.

"Take off yours." They stood up, removed their garments, and looked each other over.

"No genitals, no anuses," Saro noted. "But you still have your female form."

"And you are still wedge shaped. And I like your hair." They ran their fingers through each others' short manes.

"Your morontia hair is beautiful and lush," said Saro.

"Yours too!"

"Hair style appears to be optional here. You noticed we newborns all have the same color and length hair? But our relatives have different colors and lengths," said Saro.

"Apparently it's a choice. Everyone starts out with this."

They lay down again and observed the stars for a long while. Then Saro began massaging Kala. She did the same for him, something they had always done for each other while in human bodies. It was unhurried and especially pleasurable.

"The feelings and senses I get from this body, so far, I like very much," mumbled Saro as Kala massaged his new shoulders.

"And this is just the first of 570 body versions. Remember that from the book?" asked Kala.

"I do. Aren't there eight morontia versions or phases provided on Mansonia, seventy-one at the constellation level, and 491 more between Edentia and Salvington?"

"That's right...as I remember it," replied Kala. They were both now recalling much from *The Urantia Book*. It was the teachings of this book she had embraced as a youth, thanks to her parents. And it was those teachings that Kala and Saro studied and talked about many, many times while traveling around Urantia, distributing the book and living its teachings for over 50 years.

"Let's take a walk, Saro."

This time they exited from the lodging's back gate. It was dark out, but they had no trouble seeing under the starry sky, morontia night vision being excellent. They discovered the heavenly little park behind their abode, with crisscrossing paths, perfectly formed shrubs, beautiful statuary, an array of trees great and small spread throughout, and a broad variety of aromatic flowers of varying shape and size.

Along the paths were low walls with embedded plaques

bearing inscriptions. All were in languages they didn't recognize. Stopping at one, Kala reached out to touch it. Instantly the script translated to English. They looked at each other, smiled, and said, "Should have known!"

Saro read it, " 'Human things must be known in order to be loved, but divine things must be loved in order to be known.' Blaise Pascal, Urantia." (102:1.1)

Saro recalled, "That quote's in *The Urantia Book*. Wonder who else in Urantia's history resided in this place?" They noticed another inscription across the path. He touched it.

"This inscription is by someone from Anova, the System's oldest inhabited world. It states this being was the first to reside on Mansion One."

They lost track of time, wandering through the park, sometimes stopping and simply taking the beauty in, sometimes sitting quietly watching their passing thoughts and filing away questions. The urge to worship arrested their attention several times that night. It felt good to indulge the urge whenever and wherever they were. At times Michael's and Mother's spirits felt closer, then God's.

Passersby completely understood, because they too indulged the urge. Apparently it is universal in the humble, grateful, newly resurrected children of God.

As the pair watched their first dawn appear from atop a charming, three-tiered gazebo at the park's center, morontia animals began skittering to and fro. Colorful birds with long feathers flew, chirped, and sang. It was an unforgettable experience, combined as it was, with the growing realization of the implications of life eternal, everlasting friendship with the Universal Father, serving forever in the great cosmic family whose innumerable worlds are indeed 'cities of God.'

"Guess we'd better return," whispered Kala in Saro's ear.

"No."

She laughed. "Let's go, you bum. Aren't you curious what

the Receiver wants us for this morning?"

"I miss the kids. It could be a long time before we meet again. We may have to wait for a millennial, or even a dispensational resurrection." Saro said thoughtfully.

The short walk back to their lodging was with few words. About now the ambiance of this place was becoming evident to them; here is love, fearlessness, progress, spiritual joy and God's peace.

"No war, no weather, no wind," mused Kala.

"I feel wind just a bit once in a while," said Saro. "There has to be some atmospheric movement...but the temperature here is just right, isn't it?"

The Receiver hadn't yet arrived, and the twilight sky was irresistibly appealing, so they stopped at their lodgings back gate and sat for a moment facing each other, on a low, round, sculptured seat that was soft, but shone like polished gold.

They gazed over each other's head at the gradually dawning sky of their first full day on this paradisiacal world.

Before long the Receiver arrived at their cottage and called out. They raced around to its front entrance. Saro invited her in saying, "You are a beautiful creature, more beautiful than yesterday."

The Receiver smiled and thanked him. "Ready to go to work?" she asked.

The pair stood silent a brief moment, then simultaneously replied, "Yes!"

"Your help is needed, but certainly not required. There were several Urantian Anglophones in your resurrection group, but none have ever been exposed to the teachings of *The Urantia Book*. For some, resurrection can be a bit of shock to the soul. We were hoping you two would volunteer for a short period this morning, before your ceremonial welcome, and briefly convey your understanding of where they are, how they came to be here, and where they are going. Then answer questions that most assuredly will be asked. We have found that hearing the facts from one of their own kind sometimes helps ease the impact of transition. But you are in no way obligated, of course."

Kala and Saro immediately let her know they would be delighted to be of service in this way. They then asked about the welcome ceremony and were told it would begin this morning in the Banquet Hall, adjacent to Resurrection Hall.

"Please meet me at the hall mid-morning, at the same chamber where you resurrected. I will have the group gathered there," the Receiver said. "Between now and then, you may wish to study a chart of the being-types to be encountered on M1. And a tutorial about your new bodies might also interest you. Your harps will connect you to our central library and all archives."

"How will we know it's time to meet you?" asked Saro.

"Your harps monitor the local time beacon. Is there anything else you need?"

"No, nothing," answered Kala. Saro shook his head no.

"Thanks very much to you both. The meeting will be short. Afterwards, we will attend your formal welcoming, from representatives of your creator parents, among others. And from two of your long ago predecessors, the first souls to graduate from Urantia."

They thought for a split second, "Andon and Fonta!"

When Saro and Kala arrived at Resurrection Hall on this first morning of their first full day on M1, the Receiver led the group to a relatively quiet, semi-enclosed area where they could be seated. There she introduced the group of nineteen somewhat mystified souls (along with their assigned Receivers) to the pair. She informed them that Kala and Saro were fellow ex-Urantians who speak their language.

The Receiver went on to say, "Speaking for the Companion Corps of Mansonia One, we hope you all enjoyed the first night on our world — now your world. Your Pilgrim Receivers deliberately put off your less pressing questions until this morning, in order that you might acclimate overnight and somewhat absorb yesterday's experience before receiving instruction from one of your peers this morning.

"You have been informed Urantia is the name of the world from which you ascended?" All affirmed it.

"The mansion worlds became known on Urantia through celestial agencies present on every evolving planet, by their contact with certain men and women, like Paul of Tarsus, and John Zebedee who was an apostle of the one you may know as Jesus, who sojourned on Urantia well before you incarnated. Some of you may be recalling those teachings, teachings that were expanded upon in a little known revelatory text that Kala and Saro found early in life.

"In this Urantia Book, which was given to your former world as an epochal revelation, there is a detailed description of the seven worlds to which you have ascended. Some of you have a better idea than others about what has happened to you, because your soul was touched by Michael's Spirit of Truth that now hovers over Urantia. The name of the planet you died on is Urantia. The sphere on which you now reside is Mansion One. M1 is not made of cooling star matter like Urantia, it was built, constructed for just such a purpose as it now serves. Soul nurseries like Urantia provide a constant stream of ascenders for the mansion worlds, where your journey to God continues."

The Receiver stepped back and asked Kala and Saro to give their history with the revelatory text discovered while on Urantia, and its effect on them.

Kala related how her parents had discovered *The Urantia Book* and introduced it to her, adding, "Saro and I knew each other since childhood, but we didn't become good friends until college. It was there I talked with him about my interest and belief in teachings in the book. Almost immediately he embraced it just as I had. After school we married and spent the remainder of our lives studying and spreading its teachings, along with our work of course. We were musicians and teachers of music. We are also parents of three who are still on Urantia."

Saro added, "This book that we so treasured, and couldn't stop studying, painted a million word picture of the universe with a God of love at its center. A universe with God's descending offspring functioning as co-creators whose work it is to seed the cosmos with a broad diversity of ascending life. There are not only billions of inhabited planets like Urantia, there are billions of galaxies that have billions of stars whose planets will sooner or later bear life — life of inconceivable diversity and potential! Every part of Our Father's vast universe is under the supervision of an order of beings. Even your inner life has God at its center," he explained passionately.

They had both done this very thing many times on Urantia — introducing the teachings of *The Urantia Book* to small groups. Flashing in their minds were memories of hundreds of presentations given to a wide variety of humans during their former lives.

Saro continued, "When mortals die, they can be resurrected on another and better world — like this one. We have been reassembled in a new body/mind with our soul values intact, our original personality, and the very same fragment of God that indwelled us on Urantia. This is what has happened to all of us.

"We learned back on Earth — and you now know its true name is Urantia — of the existence of the seven mansion worlds through *The Urantia Book*'s revelations. We were taught — and we rightly believed! — that resurrected mortals take up life in a new body, and will gradually pass through all seven mansion worlds on the way to achieving perfection and sometime be embraced by God on Paradise. We're in different bodies now, aren't we? So this has to be true."

Kala then added, "We all take origin in a 'local universe'

whose co-creators are always a Michael Son and a Divine Minister. There are hundreds of thousands of local universes in the vast ring of time/space galaxies that encircle Paradise, God's home. Our Michael bestowed himself seven times across this universe, called Nebadon. He bestowed himself, in native form, from the highest to the lowest levels of our local universe. He even incarnated on Urantia, as Jesus, the last of his seven self-bestowals. The Divine Minister is his equal in creation, but they each have unique functions and roles."

Most of their nineteen hearers were stunned by all of this, but they couldn't deny they woke up in a better place with young healthy bodies, and with beings who seemed to be in charge and know perfectly well what is transpiring on this magical world. They especially liked hearing about these things from their obviously knowledgeable peers, Kala and Saro.

The group was attentive to their every word, but not grasping all that the Receiver and the pair were trying to convey. Kala and Saro continued offering revelatory details and personal insights, with the Receiver intervening as needed, explaining and reviewing that Nebadon is a creation of Michael and his mate, the Divine Minister of Nebadon. That this divine pair will eventually co-create ten million worlds with a vast and unique variety of mortal life forms to inhabit them. And that the co-creators of Nebadon are also children of the God of All Creation, now serving faithfully in the domains of time and space.

Then began a series of questions and answers. Some Kala or Saro answered, some the Receiver. This group of nineteen survivors was intensely curious, therefore good students. They had come from a variety of religious traditions of Urantia, but without exception all were happy to be alive and in this peaceful place of amazing beauty and divine appointment. None complained in the least. They were very interested in knowing more about Michael and the Divine Minister, especially the relation of Michael to Jesus. And they were informed of the greetings from ambassadors of the father and mother of

Nebadon at the banquet reception they were so soon to enjoy.

Even though the nineteen Urantia survivors had more questions for Saro and Kala, the Receiver ended the meeting in order that they not be late for the reception's beginning. As the group strolled toward Banquet Hall, more questions were asked and answered.

~ Chapter 5 ~
Banquet Hall Reception

After escorting the group of newborn pilgrims to Banquet Hall's entrance, the Receivers departed, exhorting their wards to enjoy the remainder of the day, and to be ready early tomorrow for a day of orientation.

Banquet Hall is an immense high-walled enclosure that can seat millions. It is open to the sky as are most other mansion world enclosures. Inside they found the artistry, the sculpture, the interwoven colors and decorations to be more beautiful than anything they had yet seen. Entering the massive arena with its diverse and ornate refinements was literally breath taking. Kala and Saro stopped for moment to appreciate its transcendent beauty.

As the many groups filtered in, everyone began to feel hunger in earnest, helped significantly by the smells drifting throughout the great hall. The enticing aromas flooded their minds with multiple sensations, stimulating appetites and interest in the nature and taste of morontia viands.

The dining tables were placed in rings that seated one hundred pilgrims. Each ring was reserved for a particular language group in order that a translator familiar with their idiom be present. Additional translators and guides were situated near every ring.

The hall filled with sounds of talking and laughing as the pilgrims found their way to assigned seats. Once all were in place, the Chief of Mansion One Morontia Companions ascended the raised stage at the center of the huge arena. She lifted an arm calling everyone's attention, then the other arm, signaling the beginning of the ceremony.

Suddenly a great burst of beautiful sounds seemed to fall from the sky. Morontia music emanated from everywhere. It thrilled the ears and hearts of each pilgrim in the hall. As they listened there appeared above the stage large flashing images of beautiful script rotating in mid-air, each flash in a different style. After watching many versions, one appeared with which they were familiar. Kala and Saro realized it was the word:

WELCOME!

This went on until everyone was thoroughly entranced by the mixture of music, aroma, and an artistic welcome in their own language. The whole assembly was taken up in this awe-inspiring auditory and visual experience. They felt like well-nurtured babies; God's babies.

The music softened and the Companion on stage gave another signal. Immediately circular openings appeared inside each ring of tables. Out of the openings service islands slowly arose from beneath the floor, complete with servers.

Then, more music, low, sweet, and melodious, filled the great room. The Companion bowed her head reverently. Without a word's instruction, all the banqueters and the staff did the same. The sounds harmonized well with the pilgrims' feelings of gratitude and thanksgiving. All this was being done for them. Never are there groups more appreciative of continuing life than humble planetary survivors emerging on Mansonia at the doorstep of eternity.

After a short period of thankfulness the music stopped and the voices of an unseen, heavenly chorus closed the prayer with divine intonations. These rich sounds harkened pilgrims' minds and filled their souls. When the chorus stopped and heads lifted, a moment of silence preceded the cheers and applause of two hundred thousand grateful pilgrims simply rejoicing in the gift of new life.

Before long the Companion once again drew their attention, and signaled the staff to prepare to serve the first course. The music resumed, and in strains that seem to fit this occasion perfectly. Saro and Kala were especially appreciative of the quality, power, and complexity of the music they had heard here, and at the worship service they attended after their resurrection. They wondered what sort of cello might Saro find here, and whether Kala's piano skills would be adaptable to mansion world instruments.

During the pre-banquet prayer on this, their second day, these pilgrims fresh from many worlds, rose mightily on the wings of spirit uplift. And now, they could feel a great appetite for morontia sustenance growing in their new bodies. It was a good hunger. All of them had tasted only water, and felt no hunger. Until now.

Saro remarked, "Kala, this we will remember." They toasted the occasion with water that was already set on their elegantly inlaid table, then gazed into each other's loving eyes until two staffers arrived with the first course on large, ornate trays, which they handled very skillfully. When all at their circle of tables were served, the staffers withdrew, indicating the feast should begin. The aroma was simply exquisite. The Agondonter pilgrims from Urantia were really and truly primed to begin their first morontia meal.

The first item they were served hit their palates as a bright symphony of flavors and blends. It was immediately apparent the morontia sense of taste is highly developed and exquisitely sensitive. It was cake-like with a lightness and texture they very much enjoyed, even lingering over it.

"How can food taste this delicious?" asked Saro rhetorically.

"This must be Mansonia bread," replied Kala.

After finishing the initial course of what will surely be a most memorable feast, new morontia music induced a few to dance in the open space between the ring of tables and its center service island. This music easily persuaded Saro and Kala to attempt dancing. They fairly glided in their strong, young, and able new bodies.

Most banqueters began socializing within and without their language group. An endless supply of translators was on hand, the banqueters needed only to signal for one. Laughter and joyous conversation began to echo throughout the hall in ever greater proportions, as everyone finished the first course of delightful, delicious morontia sustenance.

Saro and Kala danced like professionals under the cloudless sky. Everyone was enjoying this opportunity to socialize with the great diversity of fellow survivors, thereby keeping the translators quite busy. After their first dance as morontians, the pair joined the socializing, making several acquaintances and exchanging fascinating facts about planets of origin, about their lives and deaths as mortals. The pilgrim groups would be served seven courses before the day was over. It became obvious the courses were planned to complement and build on one another. And each course was impeccably scheduled with much time in between for mixing, dancing, and fraternal jubilation.

Well after the first course, the staff cleared the tables in preparation for the second one. After banqueters had taken their seats again, the words, "Welcome to Mansion One, Pilgrim!" appeared in mid-air directly in front of each guest, and in their language. As they marveled at the sophisticated morontia image manipulations, translators were summoned for those few who read no language.

The Chief of Companions now spoke in words that could be heard by all and simultaneously translated directly in front of banqueters. Everyone was having the same thought — Such a lovely language spoken by such a beautiful voice!

The Companion graciously congratulated the revelers on surviving and added, "What a wondrous time it must be for you all! Only yesterday you were resurrected and it appears that you have accepted this reality, if not entirely integrated it!"

A great roar of laughter came from the novice audience, at the absurd notion they could possibly comprehend any more than a small bit of what they had so far witnessed on this new world full of sounds, sights and smells of overwhelming number and diversity. But Kala and Saro were adapting quickly.

The Companion continued "You are in a good mood then? You like Mansonia food?" A mighty cheer arose.

"Thank you. Thank you all. We hope to make your welcome, and your stay, on Mansion One unforgettable, enlightening, and progressive. Countless souls have resurrected on this world, then absorbed its many lessons and moved on to Mansion Two.

"On their arrival here, all share the same desire for drink to quench their burning spiritual thirst, for food to quell their abiding hunger for Truth. We will provide everything, and you need only provide willing cooperation and joyful acceptance of the innumerable gifts of life here, created and distributed by the Universal Father and his Co-Creators who so thoughtfully provided our ground of being, a worthy purpose, and a vast universe built to give you the education required to achieve your eventual destiny, the Paradise Corps of Finaliters.

"During this day, let us fete you, let us fill you, let us welcome you and become your new friends and helpmates on this, the first step of your journey to Salvington. Beyond Salvington you will ascend to Uversa and someday take flight to Havona. And from there, go on to Paradise to meet the Father of all. Please let the staff know of any needs you have. We are here to serve, to make your time here enjoyable, fulfilling, and beneficial."

The Companion then ordered that the second course be served. A great round of applause went up. This course of liquid goodness, 'Mansonia soup,' Saro labeled it — was served and consumed to the pleasure and enjoyment of everyone. Afterward there was more dancing and broader interaction across the group as banqueters became better acquainted, recognizing that fraternal love respects no language, and knows no barriers when the children of God celebrate their progress of soul and advancement in spirit. In all their interactions the translators were extremely efficient and discrete in facilitating quality communication.

After the second course, the Chief of Companions

introduced the Archangel of Resurrection who welcomed them most touchingly. It was a welcome of utmost sincerity and divine sublimity.

She said: "I am an Archangel. It is my voice the guardians of your souls respond to in order that you may take up life again on the mansion worlds. My world, the home world of Nebadon's Archangels, orbits Michael's abode, Salvington. I have 800,000 siblings, all direct descendants of Mother and Michael. You now belong to a family of billions. When on Urantia, Michael declared: 'there are many mansions in my Father's house.' You are on the first of countless worlds that you will someday ascend to, until you stand in the Halls of Paradise and meet your Maker at the center of all things. Welcome to Mansonia, welcome to the greater family of Nebadon."

The Archangel exuded such a charming presence that it drew every eye in the hall. She went on to congratulate the survivors and encourage them never to retreat.

"And doubt not there are even greater heavens beyond Mansion One. Even heavens of heavens await those who persevere!" As she left the stage no one remained seated, all stood and applauded. And everyone wanted to know more about the Archangels.

The third course was heartier tasting to the palates of Saro and Kala, robust and filling. The artistry of the presentation well-matched the other arresting aspects of life here. The seasonings, the texture, and the aroma sent their senses to new levels.

"I can feel the energy in this food," commented Saro.

"It's more than mere food," Kala said as she ate the last of it. "Let's dance."

What a charming scene it was, this high banquet for lowly pilgrims. But they were feeling completely assured of their importance to both the workers and supervisors of this world. It was already becoming obvious to the pair that the driving motivations on Mansion One are love and service. It was palpable.

During this interlude, Saro and Kala chatted freely with others at their ring of tables. As the communal spirit rose, all were beginning to feel quite fraternal and at ease. The pair was discovering that not all of their fellows were grounded in revelation before dying. But all were well grounded in God, and intent on discovering what was expected of them now.

Between the third and fourth courses, after the audience had danced and socialized for a long while, the Companion asked everyone to be seated. She then invited a representative from the Most Highs of Edentia to address the room.

"The Most Highs send greetings and congratulations to you, resurrected pilgrims who took origin on one of the many evolutionary worlds of the Norlatiadek Constellation. Now you are the newest citizens of Mansion World One of the System of Satania, whose sovereign is Langaforge.

"Lanaforge has been entrusted to lead this System and ensure you have safe and profitable passage to Edentia. You may trust him, as we have. And now you are also members of a great family of beings of wide variety and purpose that was inaugurated by Michael and the Divine Minister far, far in the past.

"Some of you began your journey on quarantined spheres. Even with that handicap your faith carried you through to the third circle of mortal attainment. Your guardians were assigned, you died, and you were resurrected here yesterday. Quarantined or not, every one of you is to be admired and honored for persevering on the evolutionary worlds, worlds that were designed to test mortals, and to foster the formation of a vehicle worthy of the eternal voyage, even your soul.

"If you do not give up, this soul, in concert with the other aspects of your being, will someday fuse with the Divine Monitor, that prepersonal fragment of God who indwells you. You are, if you so choose, destined to become full-fledged spirit beings, ready to ascend the long stairway to the abode of God, from Mansonia to the Paradise of paradises.

"I was sent here to inform you that the Most Highs look forward with great anticipation to your eventual arrival on Edentia. When you have ascended the seven mansions, when you graduate from the schools of Jerusem, the Most High fathers will gladly welcome you to even greater mansions, to the colleges of Edentia."

The banqueters were listening closely to the representative's words. Not all understood everything that was put forth in the Most Highs' message, but Kala and Saro were gratified that they had studied the government of God as it operates on various levels of existence. They well knew of Edentia, Salvington, Uversa, Havona and Our Father's Paradise abode at the center of all things and beings.

When the Most Highs' representative finished delivering his messages, the tables were cleared in preparation for the fourth course. The mood was certainly rising among the celebrants. The great arena was filled with the beautiful sounds of morontia music and two hundred thousand new beings mingling, joyously coming to know their siblings ascenders. Some actually met the Most Highs' messenger, who descended the stage and very graciously walked among them, greeting and welcoming many individually, and as new morontians.

~ Chapter 6 ~
Andon and Fonta's Welcome

Kala and Saro noted the portions were not large, but each course was satisfying and packed a great deal of energy. Their nascent bodies were being invigorated for the first time by morontia sustenance while their minds were being filled with these first morontia experiences, the memories of which they will carry into eternity. Their souls were feeling the sublime satisfactions of new emergence and the vast potential for greater participation with and in the Adjuster. Rapid spiritual progress is at hand!

After the fourth course, the main course, was served and slowly consumed – fostering universal expressions of pleasure and exclamations of delectability – the resurrectees received another welcome. This one coming from two remarkably luminous and perfectly proportioned beings who were called on stage by the host Companion.

She embraced them and said in a touching and fraternal manner, "Most of you know of Urantia by now, number 606 of 619 inhabited planets in this System. It is so well known because it is the planet where Michael, the sovereign leader of all Nebadon and eventual father of ten million inhabited worlds, bestowed himself for the seventh and final time, incarnating in person. A million Urantia years before Michael incarnated as Jesus the first two humans emerged. They were the first on Urantia to receive divine Adjusters. Listen to their story. They long ago trod the path you are about to enter upon."

Kala and Saro well realized whose presence they now beheld. The pair was struck by Andon's and Fonta's appearance, by their pronounced beauty, poise, symmetry, their divine and sublime composure. They were seeing fused beings for the first time, ones like themselves, born as mere babes on Urantia.

"We are the ancestral parents of the human race of Urantia. I am Fonta and this is Andon. Welcome to the newest members of our ever-growing family of grandchildren who hail from Urantia. Welcome to all who ascended from the worlds of evolutionary development and soul-making, you who have endured the test of human incarnation, and come to this place for such honors as you have rightly earned. It was on this mansion that we too were resurrected. And we have since completed the course set for us by our wise leaders and able administrators. You may trust yourselves to their care."

Everyone was enthralled by the charm and gracious communications from this long-ago fused being. Fonta's words poured into their hearts and a divine kinship grew then and there. All banqueters were now realizing that fusion is their destiny too.

Then Andon spoke, "After Fonta and I completed the mansion world program and made the final choice to merge our souls with the Divine Indweller — the very same type of Indweller every one of you now host — we were granted permission to 'tarry for a season' in the System, in order that we might greet and encourage ascenders like you who have emerged as new morontia beings.

"Yours is a great destiny, and we the Adjuster-fused call out to you from Jerusem and beyond, as far as Paradise, and declare that you too can find and secure the oneness of being in eternity that is your birthright. This is our Father's intention for you. Every facility and service you will require has been created and made available. Everyone and everything here will assist you in discovering and achieving your divine destiny, to become one with your indwelling God, as we have."

The entire arena was silent except for Andon's rhapsodic voice. Most all were thinking what a worthy destiny he and Fonta have attained. The seeds of enthusiasm for the divine path born on the evolutionary worlds are now germinating in the hearts, minds, and souls of each ascending pilgrim.

Fonta added, "We would like to extend a special congratulatory welcome to the Agondonters, those of you who were born on worlds in quarantine, where the truth has been distorted and where there is no one of celestial authority to whom you might appeal, where no physical presence of a descending Son of God can be seen by the ascending mortals. Andon and I were in such a situation once. You relied wholly on faith, revelation, and your divine Indweller, your Paradise Partner, to bring you to this world, just as we did. Congratulations, well done!"

The Companion asked all Agondonters to stand and receive congratulatory applause from their fellows. Saro and Kala were reluctant to stand, but did so in their humble way, to honor the acknowledgment.

The banqueters were thrilled to see Andon and Fonta leave the stage and enter the dining area. They were followed by a large group of other sets of fused planetary parents. The couples waded in and then separated, moving singly around the hall. Before the next course was served they greeted and engaged pilgrims at every ring of tables. They personally spoke with and encouraged thousands, and seemed to grow more brilliant, charming, and beautiful as they went.

Saro and Kala watched and waited, hoping Andon or Fonta might come near. It so happened Andon and Fonta had been informed where each Urantian was seated. When it was apparent Andon was nearing their table ring, Kala decided to greet him personally. As he approached, Kala took Saro in hand and moved toward this marvelous fused being.

When the opportunity presented itself, Kala introduced herself and Saro, adding, "We also were born and died on Urantia."

"So was I," said one in the group standing near, one whom Kala and Saro had instructed before the banquet. Several others of the group then declared they also hailed from Urantia.

In a majestic and even-toned voice, with obvious and

tremendous affection, Andon replied, "You and many others, here and beyond, are family. Fonta and I know you, Kala and Saro, are parents of three. The number of your seed may someday match ours." They all laughed, and at the same time wondered if Andon knew the life story of each of his and Fonta's vast progeny, some 250,000 generations of Urantians. Then Andon hugged Kala. His gentle, loving touch brought an experience of undiluted affection that filled her to the brim, body, mind, and soul. Saro had the same reaction to Andon's embrace. Andon embraced as many as came to him.

Before departing the group he said, "Once again, and I speak for Fonta as well, congratulations and welcome."

Andon didn't appear to be in any way depleted by communing with and embracing so many. It was plainly obvious he enjoyed it, as he truly beamed with fraternal love and spirit joy. He very humbly excused himself from their group, in such a way that sent a message but without saying it, 'I don't wish an entourage to follow.' They all seemed to understand, even though some thought they had met a fully realized child of God and only wanted to be near him. It was sinking in ever more deeply that this was in their future, to become one with the indwelling fragment of the God of all Creation.

The fifth course gave the banqueters a good sampling of morontia food plants, and it was quite obviously prepared by consummate artists. The servers informed them that all of the course's ingredients were grown in the extensive gardens surrounding Banquet Hall. Kala and Saro had remarked on the gardens' beauty and organization on the way to the banquet.

This Mansonia salad was combined in a way — super vegetables and exotic tasting herbs, mixed with fragrant and spicy oils — that made it incredibly and irresistibly enticing to their morontia eyes. The ingredients were a variety of vivid colors; violet, red, indigo, brown, green, orange, and white, all beautifully arranged in various shapes and sizes. The delicate, subtle, and profound taste combinations caused nearly every banqueter to enjoy the flavors rather than talk. But not for long.

Soon there were eruptions of moans of goodness ingested, followed by universal exclamations of delight.

"At our first chance, let's tour the gardens," said Kala.

"I was hoping we could check the relatives and friends registry on our first liberty day," replied Saro.

"Of course! Then the gardens," she smiled.

'How beautiful that smile,' thought Saro.

After that exquisite, but certainly not heavy course, they felt inclined to move. Just then the music swelled, and this time almost everyone felt like dancing. The level of joy and mirth was building as all were taken up in this fascinating, memorable, once-in-a-universe-career experience.

"Who do you think will welcome us next?" asked Saro as they moved slowly to the intoxicating music. The artistry of the soundscape continuously stimulated pleasant and unprecedented moods in every one of the banqueters. It was becoming more and more obvious morontia bodies have senses and abilities that the resurrectees had only begun to discover. The pair felt strong, healthy, and focused, even as these new morontia feelings and sensations kept surfacing.

"Either Gabriel's emissary or Father Melchizedek," Kala replied thoughtfully.

After they sat and before the next welcomer appeared, Kala took off the elegant morontia shoes all pilgrims found themselves in at resurrection. She truly enjoyed bare feet and shed the slippers at every opportunity. Observing her sculpted feet, Kala declared, "Perfect for dancing."

The host Companion returned to the stage, calling attention and saying, "Throughout the Seventh Superuniverse, one class of universe sons is widely regarded as wise, those who attend to the greatest and most difficult problems that mass soul-rearing creates. So wise are the Melchizedeks that they are permitted to govern themselves.

"On their own initiative Melchizedeks patrol all the worlds of

Nebadon. Indeed they watch over every local universe in Uversa, ever available and willing to aid, assist, and enlighten wherever needed. They have never been known to be disloyal, never once in the long history of the superuniverse of Orvonton have these Melchizedek Sons ever betrayed their trust. These are your good friends and external guides. Use them!

"Nebadon has ten million of these highly versatile and loyal sons, though their work very often goes unrecognized by the creatures who inhabit the worlds they supervise. These philosophers, judges, teachers, and trainers maintain headquarters on Jerusem, the System's capital. And you will certainly pass through their 490 universities on the Superuniverse capital, Uversa. And they sometimes minister directly to the evolutionary worlds, even incarnating as ones like you so recently were. By these incarnations they lead children of darkness into the divine light of true liberty and soul progress, spirit ascension."

The host then invited the Melchizedek to address the throng.

"The Father Melchizedek of Nebadon sends greetings and felicitations to the newly resurrected children of Satania." Applause broke out momentarily. Everyone was immediately captivated by this being's bearing and presence. Saro was trying to recall how old the Melchizedek sons are. His memory was still patchy, but he did recall Michael and the Divine Minister began organizing Nebadon four hundred billion Urantia years ago.

The Melchizedek spoke eloquently and majestically as Saro and Kala shifted their gaze between him and the personalized translation that appeared before each of the celebrants.

"I was sent with this message by Father Melchizedek, the First Executive Associate of the Bright and Morning Star, Gabriel, the first born of the father and mother of Nebadon:

"We the Melchizedeks congratulate every one of you on

passing the test in the flesh. You worked diligently to gather a soul, and now you reap a reward, eternal life. You have seen some of the glories and wonders of morontia life, will you now take the last step and give God the gift of yourself? Each of you will soon make that decision.

"In all your endeavors, I urge you, do not fail to see your universe career from the highest possible perspective, always consider the cosmic outlook, Our Paradise Father's point of view which ever and anon provides the greatest good for the greatest number. You each have available a unique role in universe unfolding. You are each an indispensable thread in the tapestry of eternity.

"The challenges of the moment, the training you will receive here on the mansion worlds are the raw materials from which you will continue to gather values, spiritual values, the substance of the soul and the currency of Spirit. You are privileged to host the envy of many a universe creature, an actual fragment of The First Source and Center, Our Universe Father, the God of Paradise. After you have fused with this mighty Indweller, you will be prepared to ascend to Edentia, and eventually on to my place of origin and residence, the Melchizedek worlds orbiting Salvington.

"Between here and Salvington you sons and daughters of time and space will hear those longed for words, 'This is a beloved child in whom I am well pleased.' Heed you well the teachers encountered on the way to full universe citizenship. Listen to your instructors, and take counsel when it is offered by those of us who were designed to fill just such roles as this. You and I were created for each other, by Michael and the Divine Minister, who in turn were created by the Original Wiseman of the Universe, Our Universal Father."

This great being then summoned a large group of fellow Melchizedeks to the stage front. They too descended into the sea of banqueters. There they freely mixed, answered questions, imparted insights and established new relations between two vastly different orders of being, newly resurrected pilgrims from lowly evolutionary worlds and ancient Melchizedeks hailing from the commanding heights of Salvington and Uversa.

~ Chapter 7 ~
Sixth and Seventh Course

As the Melchizedek Sons moved toward the ring of tables to which they were assigned they paused to greet individual banqueters. When these ancient beings reached their appointed ring, they took a position at the center. When a Melchizedek entered Kala's and Saro's ring, all one hundred remained seated. The table rings were separated just enough that the voices from one did not significantly disturb or distract adjacent rings.

As a warm and fraternal greeting gesture, Melchizedek bowed to the group ever so humbly. Then he proceeded to answer all questions with good humor and unflagging charm. This period of questions and answers was the longest break between courses so far. Each answer caused his hearers to have many more questions. This superb giant of wit, charm, and grace radiated a light that could only come from a being billions of years old.

Kala and Saro listened intently but asked no questions. Very much of the truth, beauty and goodness he shared with this group of spiritual babes, this class of cosmic beginners, Saro and Kala well knew already. When he exited, everyone stood and applauded lovingly, for they had all fallen in love. Then and there an enduring interest in the Melchizedek order was integrated into the mind of each pilgrim.

The sixth course was liquid, a refined elixir that opened up whole new vistas in taste. It was slightly more viscous than water, with iridescent colors that shifted as the goblet was moved. Kala, Saro, and all the banqueters observed it in fascination for a moment but didn't hesitate to take a sip.

Their server said, "This is a combination of the juices of seven types of morontia fruit." It was slightly sweet, supremely flavorful, and very robust. It seemed to satisfy an unrealized thirst. Almost all imbibers sipped and savored it with gusto.

Just as they were finishing, the host called for the pilgrims' attention. With a charming smile she asked, "Are all enjoying?"

A tremendous roar of approval instantly flooded the reception hall. Her smile grew even bigger.

She continued, "In every local universe there is a Mother and a Father. This pair of primary procreators give life to countless individuals who inhabit millions of their evolving worlds, spiritual infants who become hosts to the Paradise Indwellers, just as you are indwelt. Sooner or later, you all crave to know your Creator Parents, your universe Mother and Father. And so you shall.

"When the Divine Minister, the Mother of Nebadon, and Michael were given this region of space to create their universe according to the plans of the Architects of the Master Universe, their first born son Gabriel worked alone. When it was time to create assistants for their son, our universe parents brought into being thousands of angels who are now known as Brilliant Evening Stars. Two of them have come from Salvington to welcome you. Always do they travel in pairs, always do they enjoy ministering to the children of Michael and the Divine Minister. It is a special honor to introduce your Creator Mother's emissaries."

With the word brilliant in their title, the pilgrims were somewhat prepared to lay eyes on the pair of beings who then took the stage. But brilliant was a vast understatement in the minds of every one of the two hundred thousand who beheld this order of being for the first time. Those who hadn't already, now realized there are many levels of being, and many kinds of beings who are teachers and toilers in the creation and administration of Nebadon's eventual ten million worlds.

A truly angelic voice entered their ears when one of the two spoke, "We hail from Salvington, with affectionate greetings from the Divine Minister. Our Mother, the Divine Minister of

Nebadon sent us to welcome her children to the first of many wombs of space. She entreats you to willingly and joyfully pass through each one, gathering what you must, attaining what you require, and then to come to Salvington, the capital of our universe of origin and the abiding place of our Creator Parents."

Her complement spoke adding, "Your Creator Mother wishes you to know that she loves you, that she adores and cherishes every one of you. And the solicitous devotion of her angels will nurture you until you are spiritually fit to advance to Jerusem, Edentia, Uversa, Havona and Paradise. Come to your Mother on Salvington, receive the milk of eternal life, let her embrace you. We, her angels, will guide you. Her sons will teach you, even as Our Father on Paradise indwells and pilots you. You cannot fail, unless you give up. And remember always, she is with us. Her Spirit pervades all Nebadon. And Michael's Spirit of Truth is ever with you. Now your Mother beckons you to the abode where she and Michael dwell."

This brought some listeners to tears of joy. These two beautiful creatures exuded a maternal-ness that plainly reflected their source, the Mother of all Nebadon's ministering angels, the distaff parent of the local universe's needful ascenders. The words of the pair struck deeply in each pilgrim's mind and heart. It helped that those words came from such luminous ones as these truly brilliant beings.

After the Brilliant Evening Stars were roundly applauded in a long ovation of deep and sincere appreciation, and finally escorted from the central stage, the host Companion signaled the service staff to bring forth the seventh course of this divine banquet, the dessert course.

Kala and Saro could smell its aroma even before being served, as if it had just been created. This strikingly attractive and artistically embellished dessert had seven layers, alternating in color between azure blue on the bottom and cloud white on top. It was perfectly round with three concentric circles, also azure, on its slightly domed upper surface. The base of it was encircled with a beautiful arrangement of aromatic flowers and lovely leaves that changed color according to direction of view, all edible. The staff of efficient servers brought fresh chilled water to accompany this gorgeous piece of food art. When all in their table ring had been served dessert, they began consuming it in unison.

As the seventh course cast a variety of flavors across their virgin morontia tongues, the pilgrims began oozing sounds of sweet delight. And more came with each bite, until nothing could be heard in the hall but one great sound of pleasure. After a moment, everyone began to laugh at the collective moan, and out of sheer joy over their now consummated welcome. They were ready to be mansion worlders.

The pilgrims had time to socialize before the final welcome. Unrestrained gaiety and fraternity filled the hall.

"What could top this feast?" mused Saro.

"Michael." Kala replied.

Not all pilgrims were familiar with the emblem of Salvington, Michael's crest. Saro and Kala informed their table-mates wanting to know if the circles on top of their dessert had special significance.

Socializing went on until the day sky began to wane. Pilgrims danced and conversed, visited other table areas, and in general thoroughly enjoyed themselves without the least self-consciousness or worry. They were all completely satisfied, without thirst, without hunger, and with a warm and loving family. They did not in any way feel heavy or lethargic. Quite the reverse, everyone was more energized than ever, as the day turned into night.

From the stage the host called the hall to order and patiently waited until all had taken their seats and ceased conversing.

"For the creation and administration of the local universes of time and space, Our Father on Paradise and his Son, the Eternal Son, provided an order of being known as the Michaels.

The Michael Sons, along with their compliments of being, Daughters of the Infinite Spirit, are designed to become co-creators and sovereign administrators of their assigned segments of space. Our segment is known as Nebadon, and Nebadon will eventually have ten million inhabited worlds, all created and managed by this pair of local Gods whose origin is the Paradise Trinity.

"Our Michael is the 611,121st being of that order of sonship, and his mate is the 611,121st being of her order. Michael's bestowed Spirit, the Spirit of Truth, is with you even now. As is the Mother of Nebadon, the provider of mind. And each of you knows of the presence of the indwelling fragments of the Paradise Father, your divine Thought Adjusters. There is a trinity of divine ministry living and working within you ascenders, ever urging you on to greater and greater heights. Father, Michael, and Mother's spirits are everywhere present in Nebadon, and they most certainly hover over you, even dwell within you."

The host then exited the stage, leaving it entirely vacant. Nothing occurred for a long moment of near total silence. The audience could sense something great was about to unfold. They remained silent. Kala and Saro glanced at each other with a smile and simultaneously mouthed the name, "Michael!"

Soon, a tall slender shaft of light appeared high over the central stage and very slowly descended. As the light widened and focalized, it grew in intensity, size, and beauty. The group's collective attention shifted entirely to that mysterious luminosity. It gradually increased in brightness and allure until the pilgrims felt this must be the maximum of visual experience.

As they sat back in awe, amazement, and fascination, a transcendently beautiful voice came to the pilgrims' ears. Some thought they heard it, some thought it occurred in their minds. A translation did not appear before them as it had previously. It was not required because the words were in the language of each hearer.

"I am the way, the truth, and the life. Follow me."

This warm presence of light then, very slowly, appeared to diffuse and expand to embrace the whole hall and all its pilgrims, service staff, and invited guests. None doubted that they were feeling Michael's embrace, his touch. Everyone realized they were experiencing a divine being of an order that hailed from a much, much higher place, a pure and holy place of unimaginable glory and splendor.

Kala and Saro were completely absorbed in the moment. They watched and felt utter bliss as Michael's luminous presence gently lifted and slowly became less and less visible, until it vanished. But none felt sorrow nor loss, for they now had in their possession the experience of an embrace with a genuine God which would remain forever theirs.

They all then recalled that this local God is but one of some six hundred thousand Creator Fathers and Mothers, each pair with their own universe. Therefore, the Paradise Father must be a Person of staggering immensity, dignity, and presence. Saro and Kala were recalling that pilgrims will certainly rise to the level of Michael on Salvington, even to God on Paradise, by the sevenfold ladder of pilgrim ascension.

When the host Companion did not return to the stage after Michael's welcome, the recently embraced pilgrims began talking with one another about that experience with him. It was so personal and unique they found it difficult to describe. But the experience was undeniable, and they had each other as co-experiencers.

Their joy was supreme, and their souls were in a state of sublime peace at the end of this, their first full day as morontian beings on M1. They had all witnessed a spectrum of unalike beings take the stage. Beings who stimulated their minds and warmed their hearts, from the Morontia Companions serving on this world, to Michael, Nebadon's Creator Son reigning over millions of evolutionary worlds from its capital Salvington.

A lovely strain of soft music was heard, apparently emanating from everywhere. It was perfect accompaniment after such a day. Everyone was virtually aglow by this time and primed to celebrate.

"Care to dance, my love?" asked Saro of his onetime wife, and mother of his children.

"Why yes," Kala replied, offering her hand.

Gradually the music swelled and rolled, and as it did, so did the mood. Kala and Saro both were wondering where in the universe there might be a more joyful occasion. Soon, almost every banqueter was dancing. The whole group felt as if they truly were in heaven. Even though it was dawning on all that the road to the highest heaven could be long and perhaps even arduous. Kala and Saro were sure of it, and wholly ready to take on the challenge.

Jubilant dancing, warm conversations and whole-hearted fraternity filled the time before their departure, notwithstanding the evening had a timeless quality. But ere long, the Agondonters from Urantia prepared to depart. As Kala and Saro were sharing hugs with new found friends and making plans to reconnect later, the host once more asked for everyone's attention.

In a most charming and loving voice she said, "And now, ascenders, go to your lodgings. Be prepared, on the morrow at daybreak, to begin your final day of welcome, Orientation Day, after which you will enjoy ten days of liberty, your time to explore Mansion One. I bid you goodnight, and once again congratulate you on resurrection and survival."

Immediately there began a chorus of heavenly voices, barely audible at first, then gaining volume until the first of three crescendos stirred the resurrectees to the threshold of prayer and adulation. Some heads bowed; kneeling felt appropriate to others, but all gave thanks for life, for a universe dominated by love, and their divine welcome to Mansonia.

Some didn't leave the Banquet Hall after the closing prayer. They remained for the night, worshiping. Saro and Kala kept dancing until the music faded, then decided to go. For the first time, they were thinking of rest. They had, after all, been in full-bore experiential mode for a day and a half, without ceasing. "That's almost five days on Urantia," Saro calculated.

Walking back to their lodging arm in arm, they talked little. They were simply taking in the fascinating sights of this magical place, now cloaked in the shadows of night. Every structure, every being, every point of light on the surface and in the sky held a special beauty, etching itself into their memories. Their bodies, minds, and souls were completely satiated. And this heaven of a world felt a bit more like home now.

They didn't go directly to their abode. They strolled the same park where they had spent the previous night. Saro and Kala wanted to add one last touch to this day's experience before terminating it in rest. They found a cozy nook from which they could view a broad swath of the park. There they sat for a long while, watching others, listening, silently communing with their Adjusters, the Divine Minister, and Michael, ever grateful to God and for each other.

After their visit to the park, Kala and Saro came home and fell into bed. As they viewed the night sky Saro said, "I'm speechless."

"Me too."

They took each other in arm and rested in that embrace for the night.

~ Chapter 8 ~
Orientation

The pair was awake before dawn. They remained in bed thinking of the day ahead, intermingled with periods of communing with the God who created the Creators who make the mansion world experience possible. They made it not only possible but inviting, thrilling, and most of all, spiritually edifying, soul satisfying.

Kala and Saro each knew when the other was in worship mode. Worship was their habit as humans, it felt perfectly natural to continue that here. Notwithstanding the many inspiring ideas surfacing in their new and marvelously efficient minds — plus the myriad attractions and powerful stimuli of this super-rich environment — worship was still their uppermost thought.

After a while Saro said, "It feels like my attachment to Urantia is beginning to slip away. You?"

"Yes, now that you mention it. But you know we'll never forget Urantia. Besides, our kids, grandkids, and great grandkids, are still there. This world is peaceful; it knows its purpose; there's a single focus. I like it because everyone is on the same path.

"There's no worry here, at least so far. No one I've met seems worried, or fearful...but I'm recalling speculating about how many, what percentage if any, give up the Paradise journey after resurrection."

"Not you, nor me, nor any of ours!" replied Saro hugging her firmly. They kissed and smiled adoringly at each other.

"Let's wake up Will, Joy, my parents, and grandparents. They're all leaving M1 today."

"That's right. Let's go," said Saro.

They leapt from bed, looked in the mirror and literally giggled in the delight of being freshly alive, then pulled on their wraps and shoes, dashed outside and playfully pranced to the adjacent lodge's doorway. Both were thinking how good their strong, light, healthy bodies felt.

They announced themselves and entered. "You're all up!" said Saro on seeing the six sitting around a wide, solid gold table.

"We're about to eat. You two hungry?"

"Not at all," said Kala. Saro shook his head no.

"Did you have your first rest last night?" asked Kala's mother.

"We did," Kala replied. "I had a vision. It was vivid and beautiful, about one resurrection after another until I reached Havona. I was in front of a huge door, knocking away. The door swung fully open and I walked in. That was it."

Saro said, "I dreamed of graduating from the last of the Melchizedek universities on Uversa. There were millions of us in the class. And our angels were standing by, ready to fly us to Havona right after graduation. We were congratulated and certified by the Ancients of Days, immediately enseraphimed, and then took off together in a mass launch!" They laughed at the dramatic way he said it.

"So you both had visions of Havona," said Kala's grandfather. "I had a similar one during my first night's rest on M1. But I was flying to Paradise, just after circling Havona's billion worlds. Then I landed on Paradise and was immediately escorted to a holding area where new arrivals wait to meet God. I was ecstatic. We met and embraced. That's all I recall."

They conversed until dawn about a variety of subjects. Saro asked questions about the similarities and differences between M2 and M3. Kala wanted to know how long each of them spent on M1. They both wanted advice about how best to spend their ten day liberty.

When the day had fully dawned, Will looked out and

noticed a visitor approaching, "Here's your Receiver, Saro."

The relatives embraced a final time. All agreed to keep in touch, and to have more reunions with more family members after Kala and Saro had settled and chosen their route to Jerusem. They exchanged fond so-longs and Saro pledged jokingly to "catch up to them in order that they might all fuse off Jerusem at the same time."

On the way to Orientation Hall, the Receiver answered questions, telling them some of what to expect on their third day as mansion world citizens, adding that they would be obligation-free at the end of the day.

Orientation Hall, like Banquet Hall, is another gigantic high-walled roofless arena linked to Resurrection Hall and the Temple of New Life. It too is surrounded by stunningly beautiful and perfectly sculpted shrubbery, large flowering plants, and a variety of spreading trees. Many of the plants had violet colored leaves, but all colors were present in one form or another. Jewels, crystals and glimmering metals were hanging from, or embedded in, almost everything on this world.

The pair was more fully realizing that art and beauty are central here, not an afterthought. The Receiver informed them the landscaped plants are not of the edible variety as are Banquet Hall's encircling gardens, all are ornamental. 'Ornate indeed!' they thought.

The same pilgrims with whom Saro and Kala had spent the previous day were pouring into the orientation arena. Each one now eager to enter this new world, each one feeling they had had a taste of Paradise reality and wanted more. It helped that they were all third circlers, beings long accustomed to following the universe's watchword — Progress!

Kala and Saro immediately noticed that Orientation Hall's interior has features of both Resurrection Hall and Banquet Hall. It is bowl-shaped but segmented into thousands of square cells instead of table rings. It too is vast, able to accommodate millions.

The Receiver told them, "I will meet you at day's end, after your last session, and escort you to the exit where you may depart on ten days liberty. Or you may wish to return to your lodging, rest, and begin tomorrow. As long as you are on M1, that will be your home." She then conveyed their seat assignment and pointed them in that direction. The three embraced and separated. Aids were stationed at cross-aisles to redirect lost or confused pilgrims.

There was a soft musical interlude that allowed time for everyone to find their place and settle. All was in readiness for a long day's instruction on orientation to a new world. What is it like outside the resurrection complex? Kala and Saro's curiosity was beyond piqued, and they were just a day away from actually experiencing and exploring this new world full of strange beings and apparent mysteries, new at least to these two hundred thousand novices.

On the instructor's platform at the bottom of the great bowl, a being took a position and indicated a wish for quiet and attention. Kala immediately recognized her as the Morontia Companion who hosted their banquet the day before. It took a moment for Saro to realize it was she.

When all was quiet, the Companion spoke, "Welcome! Anyone experience a visualization last night?" Saro and Kala watched the translation before them, and immediately heard a roaring response. They looked at each other knowingly and joined the applause.

"Happens every time," said the Companion with a big smile. After a pause she went on, "Today, we hope to give you enough information to enter Mansion One on your own. Your lodging in the Melchizedek sector will be your base, your home, until you depart for Mansion Two." Everyone was watching their translation of the Companion's words, at the same time listening to her beautiful voice enunciate the morontia language.

She continued, "There is more diversity and variety here than on the worlds you so recently left — physical, intellectual and spiritual diversity. You may be overwhelmed at first. Here on Mansonia you will find transplanted artworks from far away Havona. Some of it will be visible to you, some not. Some beings here you may see, some you can only be told about. Not because they hide, rather because you have much to learn, acquire, and assimilate. Doubt not your vision, indeed all your senses, will improve greatly as you progress.

"Permit me to quote an Archangel who very wisely stated: *'To material beings the spirit world is more or less unreal; to spirit beings the material world is almost entirely unreal, being merely a shadow of the substance of spirit realities.'* (44:0.15)

'And always, as you ascend upward on the scale of life, will you retain the ability to recognize and fraternize with the fellow beings of previous and lower levels of existence. Each new translation or resurrection will add one more group of spirit beings to your vision range without in the least depriving you of the ability to recognize your friends and fellows of former estates.' " (44:0.18)

The audience was completely silent and hanging onto each word. The Companion went on, "Some of you will be on this world only ten days. Some longer. Celestial Artisans agree to tarry in Mansonia for a thousand years of superuniverse time, at least. Yesterday you were introduced to Andon and Fonta, the mother and father of the human race of Urantia. They arrived here long ago, over a million planetary years.

"Some beings pass by the mansion worlds, those coming from spheres in the advanced stages of Light and Life. You are here to learn how to reach Light and Life within yourself, to bring your soul up to that level where it may unite, where it may fuse with the divine parent of the real you.

"While you are in Mansonia the Broadcast Directors will supply you with information and news, while the Thought Preservers will gather and store your gems of mentation. And the Morontia Recorders will capture your image. The Preservers and the Recorders store your thoughts and save your images for the archives of the morontia halls of records.

"There is a real economy on the mansion worlds, and you shall have a place in it. Here you will live, serve, learn, rest, play and worship. You will earn credits for your labors that may be used for travel, for sustenance, for any number of personal wants and needs.

"There are seven mansion worlds, and all seven are satellites of Transition World One, The Finaliters World. The Finaliters are another order of being you will encounter as you explore this first heaven. In fact, one day, you will number in their ranks. The Finaliters World and its seven mansions orbit yet another sphere, one hundred times its size, Jerusem by name. There are six other major worlds orbiting Jerusem, so-called transition worlds. Like the Finaliters World, each of those six also has seven satellites in orbit. In all, there are fifty-seven architectural spheres in the System. Jerusem, the largest, is at the center of all. It will now be your goal to become a citizen of this capital world.

"You have already become a part of the history of this System. Before you leave it your contributions and rewards will be many. Afterward, you will move up to the next level of spirit training, the 771 worlds of our Constellation, Norlatiadek, with its capital Edentia, abiding place of the Most Highs.

"In the local universe of Nebadon there are 647,591 architectural worlds. Each world is built and maintained by a vast legion of beings, many of whom you will come to know and love. And consider this fact as you build a larger concept of universe life: Nebadon is only one third complete. Nebadon has more than three million evolutionary worlds with life of some kind, and will, some far-away day, have ten million.

"No one being does everything here. There is a vibrant economy, with specialized workers for every need and ministry. While you are traversing Mansonia you will repeatedly cross paths, even collaborate with, the Vocation Builders, ones who design and construct our residences. And you will meet and interact with our numerous Supervisors of Morontia Power. They are the providers of energy drawn down from the ever-circulating currents of space, and made available to all, everywhere, and in a useful form. Many are the kinds of beings you will find here on Mansonia. And all ascenders are siblings in one great and diverse family. Many more types of beings will be revealed to you at every level of your Paradise trek.

"You will find Spornagia everywhere in the System; they constitute Mansonia's workforce, adorable super animals who are helpers on the physical level. Beginning on Mansion Two and beyond, you will find another type of being called Spironga, caretakers of everyone's spiritual needs.

"While you are here you will learn. And you may be certain your education is well-planned and carefully administered by our Celestial Overseers, beings drawn from diverse orders, ones who watch over Nebadon's many schools.

"The methods employed in many of the higher schools are beyond the human concept of the art of teaching truth, but this is the keynote of the whole educational system: character acquired by enlightened experience. The teachers provide the enlightenment; the universe station and the ascender's status afford the opportunity for experience; the wise utilization of these two augments character. (37:6.3)

"Fundamentally, the Nebadon educational system provides for your assignment to a task and then affords you opportunity to receive instruction as to the ideal and divine method of best performing that task. You are given a definite task to perform, and at the same time you are provided with teachers who are qualified to instruct you in the best method of executing your assignment. The divine plan of education provides for the intimate association of work and instruction. We teach you how best to execute the things we command you to do. (37:6.4)

"The purpose of all this training and experience is to prepare you for admission to the higher and more spiritual training spheres of the superuniverse. Progress within a given realm is individual, but transition from one phase to another is usually by classes. (37:6.5)

"The progression of eternity does not consist solely in

spiritual development. Intellectual acquisition is also a part of universal education. The experience of the mind is broadened equally with the expansion of the spiritual horizon. Mind and spirit are afforded like opportunities for training and advancement. But in all this superb training of mind and spirit you are forever free from the handicaps of mortal flesh. No longer must you constantly referee the conflicting contentions of your divergent spiritual and material natures. At last you are qualified to enjoy the unified urge of a glorified mind long since divested of primitive animalistic trends towards things material."
(37:6.6)

The Companion then gave an overview of M1's transportation system as correlated images and maps appeared beside her. The professionalism of the mansion world administrators very favorably impressed Saro and Kala.

Next she instructed the group on using their harps to obtain information of every imaginable kind, to find individuals, and to locate places. She then asked a company of Mansion World Teachers, who were already in place and standing by in each occupied square, to begin a question and answer period for their group. Kala recalled these teachers are 'abandoned' angels, cherubim and sanobim whose former wards have gone on to Edentia.

This pattern of offering general information from the instructor's platform, then following it with question and answer sessions about specifics, led by two Mansion World Teachers within each square, repeated all day. The pilgrims were loaded up with useful advice on ways of doing things, and ways not to. The Companion showed them charts of the types of beings here, some of which Kala and Saro had examined the previous morning at their Receiver's suggestion.

Around midday the Companion sent the group on break, for sustenance, for rest, for worship; however they wished to spend it.

Saro and Kala spent the break strolling around the outsides of all three halls, enjoying the aesthetics of morontia gardening alongside and integrated with shimmering and bejeweled architecture. Most structures, art, and sculpture were made from lustrous morontia materials that well resonated with their quickly expanding sense of aesthetic appreciation.

Kala spotted a group of spornagia tending the gardens. They moved closer, pausing to watch the creatures working, and quickly confirmed Malavatia Melchizedek's statement about their extraordinary beauty and a Bright and Morning Star's description of these lovely and useful morontia animals. She wrote in part:

"...They are devoted to the care and culture of the material phases of these headquarters worlds, from Jerusem to Salvington. Spornagia are neither spirits nor persons; they are an animal order of existence, but if you could see them, you would agree that they seem to be perfect animals." (37:10.3)

During the last half of orientation day the pilgrims were presented with the fundamentals of morontia culture, a culture "designed and built for transition," said the instructor. But many of them were surprised to hear her declare, "If your new body should be injured, you will be taken to one of many care facilities on M1. Yes, your morontia bodies may be strong, but they are not invulnerable. They may be injured by mishaps of *'a mechanical nature.'* " (50:3.3)

The pilgrims were also informed of the eight body changes, morontia adjustments, to be experienced during the mansion world ascension, and that there will be a total of 570 alterations by the time they ascend to Salvington.

They also learned about the world they were standing on, its overall construction from the core to the sky; the regulation of its water and its atmosphere; its power supply and distribution system including some of the beings involved in building and maintenance. They received information about the Mansonia economic system and the wide variety of service venues transient pilgrims may choose from. Practically everyone had questions about their next step after ten days of liberty.

The Companion dwelled on the real purpose of the seven mansion worlds: Spiritual progress and the shedding of the *"mark of the beast."* (47:9.1) Pilgrims who hadn't already realized it, learned that the mansions are rehabilitation worlds, a planned and well ordered system of spheres designed to orient all categories of beings coming up from the evolutionary worlds ascending into cosmic reality, and beginning the Paradise journey.

She went on explaining that, "The mansion world regime fully compensates for the lack of higher spiritual training on the evolutionary worlds. Eventually mansion worlds will no longer be needed for rehabilitation, when all one thousand evolutionary planets of the System have achieved the highest level of Light and Life.

"You passed through spiritual infancy during your former life, and now you find yourself here on Mansonia about to enter primary school. When you leave Jerusem for Edentia, you will be graduate students. And by the time you reach Michael on Salvington, you will be fully fledged, Adjuster fused, sons and daughters of God, well on the way to Uversa and Havona. And some wondrous day you will receive the ultimate degree. You will meet and be personally embraced by the Universal Father in his abode on Paradise."

In the question and answer session that followed the Companion's plenary speech, Saro used his harp to access the System's library and retrieve a line from *The Urantia Book* he couldn't quite recall word for word, and read it to the group in his study square.

"...On the mansion worlds the seraphic evangels will help you to choose wisely among the optional routes to Edentia, Salvington, Uversa, and Havona. If there are a number of equally advisable routes, these will be put before you, and you will be permitted to select the one that most appeals to you. These seraphim then make recommendations to the four and twenty advisers on Jerusem concerning that course which would be most advantageous for each ascending soul." (48:6.5)

Much useful and fascinating information was given the pilgrims on this afternoon, so much their minds felt saturated. Even Kala and Saro were taken aback by the intricacies, facilities, and provisions of this one world. And from what they had seen and felt, it is a true poem of living harmony. The host Companion thanked and dismissed the group just before eventide, right after a touching and satisfying group prayer that included a moment of worshipful reflection on the day's experiences.

When the meeting ended the pilgrims moved en masse to Banquet Hall where the service staff had set out a moving buffet. Diners could choose from a tremendous variety of dishes, all works of art, and all perfectly keyed to the morontia palate. Saro and Kala enjoyed a leisurely dinner, talking with newly made friends, getting to know this diverse family from many evolutionary worlds now gathered for the first time on a mansion world.

When the pair had finished their second delectable meal as Mansonians, Saro asked the inevitable question, "Shall we make our exit tonight, or rest first and leave early tomorrow?"

~ Chapter 9 ~
Meeting Solonia, First Transport

Just as Kala and Saro were leaving Banquet Hall, still discussing their first visit to the world outside the resurrection complex, all four of their Guardian Angels appeared.

The angels seemed even more beautiful than either of them recalled from their last face-to-face. They were both thinking perhaps their morontia vision is improving, possibly becoming better attuned to the sights and beings of this world.

"We have your assignments," said one of Kala's Guardians. "In ten days you will advance to Mansion Two."

Kala and Saro were surprised and didn't know quite how to react at first. They had erroneously assumed M1 would be their home for a while. As the implications began to dawn on them, questions arose.

"Will we stay on M2 for only ten days?" Saro wanted to know, "how far will we be advanced?"

"That we should know after you have arrived on M2, if not sooner," answered the Guardian. This meant they had just ten days to explore M1, a world the size of Urantia. Their angels led the pair to a sitting area under a giant tree by the side of the pathway, in order to discuss their plans for the coming ten days.

"We have been exploring this world during your reception and orientation," one of Saro's angels told them. "We recommend you take excursions to various sites with the aid of a personal Morontia Companion." Saro immediately thought of the Urantia Paper's revelations about excursion supervisors, Morontia Companions who serve as mansion world guides and associates in leisure.

"We four have discussed the matter, and we advise that you retire for the night and rest. We have arranged for a personal Companion to meet you at your abode at daybreak tomorrow. Of course you are not obliged to accept our arrangement, and you may change it at any time. You may leave now, and go wherever you please for the next ten days without restriction. And you will always have the option to take group excursions that leave from the Melchizedek sector each day."

Kala and Saro looked at each other, thinking for a moment.

Saro asked, "If we go with a personal excursion guide, where will she take us?"

His angel answered, "If you approve, you will be taken to the hall of records to consult the registry about your predecessors, those still on M1 who you may wish to call upon and make plans to visit during your brief stay here. Then you may wish to transport to three of the principal temples of M1. You may want to tour the seven major circles of the Morontia Companions, and view their magnificent temple. After that, you might choose to see the governor's abode. And you have already expressed a desire to visit the gardens of the Banquet Hall. But you may, if you wish, alter this itinerary at any time, at any point in your ten day liberty."

"How many days will that itinerary take?" asked Kala.

"Much depends on you, Saro and Kala. If you choose to be escorted by a personal guide, you can move at your own pace. If you choose to explore by group excursion only, you will of course forfeit autonomy. But you will have peers to share the experience. We recommend you employ both the personal guide and the group excursion options in your explorations."

Saro and Kala wanted to think over their choices, especially now, after having learned they are to be on M1 only ten more days.

The Guardian added, "Remember that all plans are tentative, you may alter or amend them at any time."

Their angels followed as the pair walked slowly toward the Melchizedek sector discussing the matter.

"Having a personal companion and guide seems like a luxury," Kala said.

"There's no shortage of luxury here," Saro replied. "And I like the idea of having someone with us who knows the territory and probably more than a few languages."

Kala agreed. Turning to the angels she said, "We prefer a personal escort, with the option to take excursions."

Saro's Guardian said, "Your personal Companion will call on you shortly after daybreak." She and the other three angels wished the pair good night, then embraced and assured them, once again, that their angels are ever at hand.

The pair went to their lodge contemplating who they might find in the personnel registry on their first day of liberty on this astonishing world with so many beings and things completely and utterly new to them.

Their personal Companion arrived on schedule at daybreak. Kala and Saro were silently worshiping in back of their abode, on an elaborate swinging platform that hung from a large flowering tree. Once they set the swing in motion and took a seat, momentum kept it swinging for a long while. As they slowly swung, drifting in and out of prayer and worship, petals fell from the tree's bountiful flowers. They were feeling a consuming oneness with Our Father, Michael, and Mother.

The Companion caught a glimpse of the pair in the swing and walked around the cottage to greet them. In soft voice she asked, "Ready to tour Mansion World One?"

They opened their eyes a bit and smiled, both uttering the word, "Yes!"

The Companion stepped forward and very graciously introduced herself, "I am Solonia."

Kala and Saro dismounted the platform and greeted her with an embrace. She was as lovely and warm-hearted as any

Companion they had so far encountered.

"That name sounds familiar," said Saro.

"Solonia was the name of the 'voice in the garden' of Eden on Urantia," replied Kala.

"I adopted that name — one that most ascending pilgrims can easily pronounce — after hearing of the loyalty and leadership she displayed while serving with Adam and Eve on Urantia."

Solonia went on to tell the pair about her title and mode of service, "My current assignment is with the Excursion and Reversion Supervisors. I have been assigned as your guide, to escort you wherever you wish to visit on Mansion One. And your Guardians informed me of their recommendations, to see the registry, to tour three of the main temples and the governor's headquarters, to visit the seven circles of the Companions, and your desire to tour the gardens of Banquet Hall."

"When may we leave?" Kala inquired with an enthusiastic smile.

"Now" said Solonia. "The registry edifice is not far from the nearest gate. And that gate is only a short walk from here. Shall we?"

"Please, lead on Solonia," said Saro. The pair was primed for this experience, ready to see just what's out there on this beautiful sphere, one of millions of "cities of God," hanging in space.

On the way to the gate, Solonia prepared them for their first impression of greater M1 saying, "You are about to view a world that leaves many pilgrims awe-struck. Since you were somewhat prepared by the revealed text you found on Urantia, you may be merely breathless," she said with a reassuring smile. They laughed, which broke any tension Kala and Saro were feeling on this unique occasion.

They were realizing that the resurrection complex is much larger and grander than they first thought, and completely surrounded by a high wall with a broad promenade on top.

There are entry and exit gates at regular intervals all around the base of the complex's circular wall. The gate they were approaching is gigantic and somehow, by its design, conveyed a sense of welcome. Certainly not foreboding.

Well before the pair came to the gate, they could glimpse activity on the outside, on the surface, and in the sky. Beings were moving about, some walking, but most riding in, or on, a variety of swift moving vehicles, wheel-less pods made of an astonishing array of materials, sizes, and shapes. All vehicles appeared to be riding on invisible currents.

Kala and Saro looked at each other with a new sense of glee and joy. It was hard for them to imagine exactly what this world would be like, but no longer did they have to use imagination. It was unfolding before them.

Their eyes became larger with every step. Already they could see a vast cityscape, with walls that form concentric circles, triangles, rectangles, and squares. When they passed through the great gate, Solonia directed them to a high lookout point that provided an unrestricted view. Just as they reached the top, Kala pointed overhead and exclaimed, "Saro, a passenger bird!" Saro looked up to see two great wings flare as a huge morontia transport animal landed with a passenger on the promenade directly above their exit gate.

What high adventure, what wondrous sights, what a world! Saro and Kala stood atop their perch, viewing the myriad complexes of work and living, with beings moving in every direction, on the ground and in the sky. The complexity and beauty of the view was all but overwhelming. The scenario prompted them to try to imagine what might be transpiring inside all those geometric formations, and at the same time wondering what it would be like to see them from a bird's back.

After seeing the big bird land, Kala and Saro glanced at each other and instantly knew one of them had to ask. Kala did so, "Solonia, are new pilgrims permitted to ride them?"

"You are," she replied.

"Today?" asked Saro.

"Now if you wish. Shall I make a reservation?" Solonia pointed to a peak on the far-away horizon saying, "That is where the birds roost."

These lovers of flying, who were both licensed pilots on Urantia, who even died while flying, were thrilled by this chance to soar on a bird's back over M1. When on Urantia they also enjoyed flying gliders for recreation and inspiration, riding on rising air currents with the soaring birds.

Immediately after Solonia made the reservation, their transport vehicle arrived. It moved very fast, dropping from the sky, coming to a smooth halt directly in front of them, then hovering silently hand-high off the surface.

One side of it opened wide and Solonia said quaintly, "Pilgrims first."

They smiled and stepped in. The vehicle held quite firm, not shifting at all with their added weight. All three took forward-facing seats on lavishly decorated bench chairs, each with cushioned and embellished armrests. They watched the door close quietly and seamlessly.

The pilotless transporter lifted off, slowly at first, then accelerated quite rapidly. Kala and Saro's morontia bodies and minds were sensing and cherishing the liberty of flight on this new world. New to them at least.

Solonia was very much enjoying watching their reactions to this first flight in a common transport pod. There were many other pods flying above and below, all perfectly coordinated apparently. The floor of the vehicle was completely transparent. Looking down in every direction there appeared dynamism, intense activity. Everything had a pristine cleanliness about it, the air, the structures, even the creatures of this world gleam with morontia beauty, purity, and appeal.

The pair was fascinated by the strange and fascinating world below, viewing it through the clear shell of their swift ride, now moving extremely fast.

"Up to 500 Urantia miles per hour," Solonia told them. They could see many interconnecting waterways and reservoirs shimmering in the early morning light. Saro and Kala were each silently expressing profound gratitude to God for this wondrous world, and for being part of it. The transport reached their destination so quickly the pair didn't have time to ask Solonia questions about all the beings and doings passing beneath them.

The pod slowed as it approached the massive aviary, sitting on top of a high, broad, pedestal formation. Just before setting down they watched birds landing and taking off. They could see that the morontia animals had stalls behind each launch point which were situated all around the pedestal's periphery.

The great birds could launch or land themselves from any point on the pedestal's edge, and retire to their appointed stall as needed for sustenance, grooming, and rest between flights.

Kala and Saro followed Solonia to their assigned transports, walking through a charming garden of low, purple-leaved trees, many laden with morontia fruits of diverse colors and sizes.

"The birds are very fond of the fruit," Solonia told them.

Their eyes bulged and their jaws dropped on seeing the gigantic birds face to face. As they approached these two great flying creatures they couldn't help but notice how intelligent and aware they appear. The birds are also beautiful, with flawless feathering, some iridescent, but mostly golden. The two giants looked alike to Saro's and Kala's untrained eyes.

As the three drew near and stood under the two birds' attentive eyes, each bird watching them out of their right eye, Kala looked up and asked the nearest one, "Do you have a name, beautiful?"

Solonia translated a jewel-ringed plaque on the roost's wall, "They are called, in Urantian English, 'Faithful-One and

Faithful-Two.'"

"That's reassuring," said Saro laughing. Solonia translated the rest, "One is male, Two is female. The female can be distinguished by a faint red band around her upper neck." Looking closely they spotted it.

In a display of friendliness and affection, the great birds slowly lowered their heads, placing their large beaks directly in front of Kala and Saro. The pair looked the animals straight in the eye and then, impulsively, indulged an urge to embrace the beasts' beaks. As they did, the birds made a chortling sound, one of approval they presumed. Saro and Kala instantly loved these giant flying animals.

After passing Solonia's brief tutorial to ensure the two possess the skill and confidence to ride the birds, she said, "Faithful-One and Two, and their progenitors, have flown this area for many generations, safely taking millions of pilgrims for their first post-resurrection flight. They know the area and will fly you to any destination their caretakers ask. The birds are quite smart and understand their keepers' language. It is advised that you not attempt to direct the bird's path, at least not until you have been qualified by the creatures' caretakers. Shall I have them instruct your birds to circle this area three times and leave you at the hall of records? We can reconnect there."

They agreed. Solonia spoke to the keeper and the keeper spoke to the birds in odd, brief spurts. The birds appeared to perceive his meaning. It was touchingly beautiful to watch them communicate. The keepers informed Solonia that the birds would be ready to launch as soon as they are outfitted.

Saro and Kala were very curious about what they only glimpsed on the way to the great pedestal, so they walked out to its edge for a standing-still view. They wanted to know more about the many activities happening inside and outside these curious triangles, circles, rectangles, and squares. The range and acuity of morontia vision continued to amaze them; they could view far away objects with astonishing clarity in detail and color. They then and there pledged some part of their ten days' liberty to tour the surface; to visit the ordinary places of M1.

When the trio returned to the birds, the keeper informed Solonia they were almost ready to mount and launch. One of the lovely spornagia came out of the stable's quarters carrying safety equipment, and offered help putting it on and adjusting it properly.

Solonia advised Saro and Kala, "The safety devices will deploy automatically should the bird, for any reason, fall from the sky. Accidents are extremely rare, but have occurred," she added.

Saro and Kala didn't seem at all fazed by any possible risk. But Kala had been wanting to ask, "Are these bodies killable?"

~ Chapter 10 ~
The Flight and The Registry

In answer to Kala's question Solonia said, "You may recall that the body you now inhabit is the same type in which Jesus was resurrected. Any morontia body may be considered beyond repair by some rare and extraordinary misfortune, but *you* will never be so regarded. Once resurrection takes place, eternity remains available to all who will persevere to the apex of the ascension scheme — Paradise perfection. And always will you have a suitable form to inhabit.

"However, Companions are instructed to advise ascenders it is intended that you use your body for the utmost benefit of spiritual progress, without putting it in undue jeopardy. One of the initial signs of spiritual maturation is the proper care and safeguard of the temple you inhabit, a gift from our creator parents, which in turn is a gift from the First Source and Center. You both did well as stewards of your Urantian bodies, as your life records show, no doubt a contributing factor to your uncommon – uncommon for present day Urantia at least – attainment of the third psychic circle before death."

Solonia confirmed what Kala and Saro already knew in their souls, that nothing good ever perishes, most especially the hard-earned values that are the sum and substance of an immortal soul.

She added, "There are time-tested systems of safety in every endeavor of Mansonia culture. But you must surely have in some manner realized the beings and forces that created your bodies can create another. And you have been told of the eight adjustments your bodies will undergo as you pass through the System."

Her answers were very much what the pair expected. But at a time like this, when one is about to dive off a high perch into an unknown world on the back of a newly-met creature, such questions do come to the minds of ex-mortals.

Their birds were equipped with a broad seat, strapped securely to the crook of their neck by colorful, highly visible webbing. The saddles have a waist belt attached at back and front, with two short hand grips in front of the saddle for passenger stability, and where reins to each side of the bird's bridle are secured.

The keepers asked Solonia to remind the passengers not to use the reins. Which she did. The pair expressed assurance and gratitude to the keepers. Obviously, the animals were in perfect condition, well cared for, and superbly content. They also exuded a powerful presence, as if their consciousness equaled the size of their body.

The keepers then led the birds to the launch point, where they lowered themselves to allow their passengers to mount. Kala and Saro donned the goggles that were offered by the attending spornagia, then climbed atop their birds; Saro on Faithful-One, Kala on Faithful-Two. They indicated readiness. The birds stood up, the keepers signaled all is prepared for launch. The animals hobbled to the pedestal's leading edge, stretched their wings and without hesitation dove nearly straight down catching the heated air coming up around the great pedestal. A favorite line from *The Urantia Book* was flashing in both their minds at this instant: *"Even when the air currents are ascending, no bird can soar except by outstretched wings."* (91:8.9)

As the pair descended and watched the surface rise, they held tightly to the saddle posts, grinning like ecstatic children, completely trusting of these giant birds and their trainers. When sufficient air speed was attained the two birds began flapping their great wings, turning upward against the warm, ascending three-gas morontia air. They rose mightily with every flap.

The birds quickly climbed in small circles to a great height above the launch point. They simultaneously stopped flapping, stretched out their giant wings, and began a gradual downward glide three times around the area that Kala and Saro had zipped across earlier in the transport pod.

The pair glanced and laughed at each other as they soared over this magnificent world. As far as they could see, there are endless activities inside and outside great circles, squares, rectangles, and triangles.

Many other beings were flying in a variety of transports around, below, and above them, including other birds with and without passengers. Transportation on the ground and in the air was a moving vision of light and life to Kala's and Saro's new morontia eyes. For a moment Kala thought she heard celestial music coming from above. Maybe it was only the wind passing her ears.

The birds were given wide berth by the powered vehicles, which made the pair realize this grand symphony of activity is composed and perfectly coordinated by unseen hands on unknown controls. As they floated slowly downward, steady on the backs of their steeds of the air, Kala and Saro were all but mesmerized by the sights and sounds of this wonder-filled world below, humming with life and best of all, full of Godliness. The urge to gratefulness overtook them both even as they satisfied this past life wish to soar on a Fandor's back.

As the pair observed the surface, they noted the many walls separating and defining the various physical features, some high and some low, some wide and some narrow. Most had shining metallic promenades on their top surface, lined with artistry and accented by sculpture. And all are studded with aesthetically appealing arrangements of reflective diamonds, great emeralds, multi-colored jewels, and precious gems in beautiful and symbolic array, some that could only be discerned from high above. In fact, their versatile morontia vision could discern large and small details on M1's surface, even from this lofty height.

Saro and Kala could see an endless web of water canals crisscrossing each of the geometric segments. Many parks, all teeming with movement, are situated along the canal's banks.

As ever on Mansonia, most structures are open to the sky.

There are also graceful spires and tall edifices dotting the landscape, but no significant land elevations or depressions to be seen, and never does a cloud appear in the rich, rich air.

Kala was looking at one of the highest points on a far-away horizon, wondering if it might be the angels' spaceport. Saro was watching Kala, her magnificent morontia self astride a beautiful bird on their third full day as resurrected ex-Urantians, now flying over the first mansion world. Their birds seem to be enjoying Saro and Kala's enjoyment. A cross species friendship was growing with each circle they made over the area.

As they flew, an even broader realization of how wonderful the rest of this world might be, hit them. And yet M1 is only the first step on the long, long, Paradise journey. Always will Kala and Saro remember Faithful-One and Faithful-Two, marvelous animals who took them on a physical flight preparatory to their imminent spiritual journey, soaring through the seven mansion worlds on the way to Jerusem.

By the time their final lap was complete, Kala and Saro were beaming with the quiet joy of a long awaited pleasure now satisfied. They glanced at each other, simultaneously thinking of attaining certification in order to make autonomous flights.

After the third circle of the area, the birds slowly glided onto a raised landing pad atop the hall of registry, flaring their great wings and settling gently. It was busy but not crowded. Land and air vehicles were coming and going on the surface below. Many other big birds were landing on and launching from the pad, with and without passengers. Holding stalls are located in a large ring at the center of the pad for the animals' comfort during waits for their passengers.

As the beasts crouched down to allow Kala and Saro to dismount, Solonia greeted them with a smile, saying, "Let me guess, you want to earn pilot's certification."

They laughed. "Where do we apply?" asked Kala.

Before departing the birds and their passengers embraced,

arms around beaks. The great beasts looked them in the eye, chortled their affection, then toddled to the edge and flew away home.

"The registry's entrance is this way," said Solonia, directing them to a shaft at the pad's center.

Saro and Kala were in awe of the fact that they were going to enter the registry they had so often read about, and even dreamed about while on Urantia. They each had short and long lists of friends and loved ones who might have preceded them. Also, they both wondered if they might discover the status of certain deceased luminaries of Urantia's unique past, beginning with Mary Magdalene, Beethoven, Shakespeare, Lao Tse, Mary and Joseph, any of Jesus' siblings, John the Baptist, Rodan, Onamanalonton, Ikhnaton, Siddhartha, and a host of others. But they had only ten days and a whole world to explore.

The hall of records was throbbing with activity, much like the rest of M1. Upon entering the shaft at the center of the hall's landing pad, the trio stepped into a tiny open-topped transport that took them down and over to the personal kiosk Solonia had reserved.

As Kala and Saro rode along, they noted the registry had many levels and categorical groupings. They also encountered beings of immense variety, hue, shape, and size, all coming, going, or busy researching. The little pods negotiated turns with ease, traveling in established corridors with other transports, peeling off here and there to leave or retrieve passengers.

After their thrilling sky ride, Kala and Saro were once again feeling the enormity of the experience of M1. Kala felt compelled to proclaim, "This whole world is a sublime work of art and heavenly beauty, an intricately carved gem hanging in space by loving command of the Deities."

Saro and Solonia smiled at Kala's poetic expression, Saro adding, "And their faithful Companions do ever lead their charges o'er this Gem, and onto the next Gem of Wonder, greater still!!" They laughed, which helped bring them down to the ground, out of the sky, to be here seeking information about enduring personal relationships, relationships that will last forever and extend all the way to Paradise and beyond, but had their beginnings on the lowly worlds of time and space.

After relaxing a bit in their comfortable kiosk with Solonia at their side, the pair began to feel as if they were an integral part of the artistry that characterizes Mansonia. They simply sat for a moment to enjoy their role in the morontia integration of living and static art, the creative intertwining of beauty in both spirit and material. The harmony of M1, the fraternity and friendliness of it, enthralled these newborns so recently from a disharmonious sphere, a sphere with humans longing for truth, starving for beauty, thirsting for love, and virtually clueless about this magnificent mansion world to which they might soon ascend.

Kala was now recalling reader conferences on Urantia that had mansion world parallels; a generalized, loving, and warm ambiance, above all else. Saro thought it correlated somewhat with the, "Christmas Spirit" of Christian tradition on Urantia, when for a short season love and kindness flows more easily, more abundantly.

Kala, Saro and Solonia spent the rest of the morning going through endless records about relatives in their blood lines, all of which had numerous connections to other records, all fascinating and revealing of lives about which they knew nothing. Solonia helped them better formulate their requests to suit the registry's retrieval system. Whatever they wished to know, that immediately appeared before them in mid-air in text, image, or graph form.

But they were surprised to discover none of their Urantia acquaintances had yet arrived, except of course the relatives who attended their resurrection, Saro's brother Will, his two cousins, Kala's parents and grandparents, and her cousin Joy. All others were either still living, awaiting dispensational resurrection, or had already graduated from Mansonia.

They each followed their lineage back to Andon and Fonta. Many in their line had attained Adjusters and passed through the mansions long ago, and some of those had distinguished themselves in service on Urantia and on Mansonia. But all had already moved up to Edentia or above.

Saro found an archive of brief messages left behind by thousands of leaders and destiny reservists who had ascended from the 619 worlds of the System. Some of them were on their lists of Urantian luminaries to look up. They spent much of the day combing through those brilliant and heart-warming greetings, along with biographies and selected thought gems of the great beings, artists, and teachers who took origin on the evolutionary worlds. The translation of the messages was almost flawless. Solonia's kind and patient assistance, along with her immense knowledge of the System's worlds, helped them greatly when any question arose.

Kala found personal messages, and recordings, of new compositions by Beethoven, Mozart, and others who reapplied their talents during the mansion world stay and left behind inspired and improved creations for fellow ascenders' enjoyment. They briefly listened to samples she discovered. There was so very much to read, view, hear, and experience just in the registry. So much so they lost themselves in it. Before they realized it the day had slipped away.

Finally Saro noted the day's passing and said, "We could spend our entire liberty here, and still only begin."

"True. Ready to take a break?" Kala answered.

"I am. Is there a temple near?" Saro asked.

"There are several inside the registry, two nearby," replied Solonia. "Shall I summon a transport?"

"If they are close, let's walk," said Saro. Kala nodded agreement. They were both sensing an urge to commune with the God who conceived the vast stupendous cosmos, replete with ancient and well-kept records, of which they have now had only a slight glimpse.

They invited Solonia to join them in worship.

~ Chapter 11 ~
Dinner And A Concert

The urge to worship is a summons to which Kala and Saro harkened several times daily while on Urantia, circumstances permitting. So much so it became an integral part of their being, ever expanding as they aged. Their call to commune was deeply affected by understanding the revelations about its central role in the lives of ascenders. And so they taught their children and grandchildren.

Already had they worshipped several times as resurrected beings. Indeed, it was their first activity after resurrection on M1. Now they are about to enter a morontia chapel inside the mansion world registry. They were very pleased to discover that worship facilities are provided, that worship is encouraged, respected, even revered here.

"It is very refreshing to find such robust sensitivity to worship," Solonia said softly, adding, "and worshiping with two Adjusted ones like you brings it additional depth and quality. So many who arrive here have little to no understanding or appreciation for it. Of course all pilgrims well know, and greatly benefit from, worship by the time they reach M7."

The three stepped gently as they found a place amid many seated, supine, and fetal-positioned morontians already in deep worship, assisted by the low, quieting harmonies that pervade the temple. Saro and Kala settled and enjoyed a timeless period communing within, with Solonia sitting between them.

Before dying on Urantia, the pair had worked aggressively, together and alone, to cultivate an intimate relationship with their respective Indwellers, wherever they were, whatever they were doing. All the while they were putting revelation into action, serving fifty years as living disseminators and advanced teachers of truth, always informed and directed by insights born of worship.

Kala and Saro had long ago learned to harmonize service and worship. They experientially understood these two activities are true delights of the soul. Worship and service foster the spiritual values that lead eventually to eternal fusion of soul and Adjuster, the joining of eternal and infinite God with the child of time and space. While on Urantia, the pair had met conflict after conflict, problem after problem, with unflagging energy and inspiring enthusiasm that came out of worshipful communion with their Paradise Partners, always aided by prayer, and the enlightened ministry of angels.

The day was almost gone when they exited the temple. The first shades of darkness could be seen in the Mansonian sky. Saro and Kala were feeling thirst and hunger. Solonia led them to nearby, diamond encrusted water founts, and asked, "Should I call for transportation?"

After looking at one another Kala asked Saro, "My love, do you want to go out on M1 for dinner tonight?"

He smiled and nodded, then invited their beautiful companion, "Stay with us. In fact, take us to your favorite place for dinner and dance. You do dine and dance?"

"I do," answered Solonia, "and it would be an honor to accompany you." A great fraternal love among these three began in earnest during their joint worship session.

A registry transport carried them to the nearest exit. They then took another vehicle high and fast, but not far, to a charming spot on the banks of a narrow canal. The transporter dropped them at the water's edge and took on four new passengers, then quickly shot off into the dusky sky.

They were early for dinner. In fact they were the only patrons or wait staff in evidence at the moment. The trio took a table under a large, flowering tree. It had long, slender, curvy branches reaching out all around, each one festooned with great clumps of bluish-violet flowers protruding wildly in every direction. Its fruit attracted a variety of morontia birds whose gentle chirping provided a natural musical background.

It was an enchanted scene, accompanied by the delicate fragrance of so many trees and shrubs displaying gorgeous and prolific flowerings. The movement of the birds caused a petal to fall on Kala's hair.

Saro took it and sniffed the delicate aroma. "Smell this."

She swooned a bit, then tasted it and said, "Mmm, tastes even better than it smells."

The power and richness of the smells on M1 delighted Kala; she was ever seeking the ultimate aroma on Urantia. Saro was also appreciating newly discovered levels of olfactory sensitivity, recalling and comparing his first scents of M1, on resurrection day.

They watched the pedestrians strolling both sides of the canal and observed watercraft moving along, some by oar power, some larger, self-propelled craft were obviously transporting excursion groups. Saro and Kala could not help but note the diversity of morontia forms of being.

"I keep noticing the great differences between morontia bodies," said Kala. "It made me think of revelations about them, a line that mentioned personal appearance here faithfully resembles the inner being."

Saro called up the text and read, *"...in the morontia life, and increasingly on its higher levels, the personality form will vary directly in accordance with the nature of the inner person."* (112:6.3)

Solonia replied, "You have been rightly informed that mortals leave nothing behind on the world of nativity except their old bodies and minds, that you retain the same level of personal and soul development in the transition from mortal death to morontia resurrection."

Kala said, "I can sense the whole, inner person in some. But in others, I sense...incompletion."

"I can too," Saro said. "Some radiate beauty, like Kala," he smiled at her, and she pointed at him. "And some appear to have beauty, but it is blocked in a way, it is partial. Yes, incomplete."

Solonia answered, "You both have ample self-awareness and enough aesthetic sensitivity to realize your morontia bodies are comparatively beautiful. All morontia bodies are alike at first. Gradually, but often rapidly, the morontia form takes on the proportions and inner nature of the being who inhabits it.

"It is obvious to my order of being — who have escorted millions of ex-mortals over and across M1 — why ones like you are not to be detained here. You both reflect an uncommon maturity and willingness to learn, to grow, to progress, along with a rare ability to effectively teach what you have learned. So your personal beauty of being has not diminished since your resurrection, quite the opposite in my estimation. It has expanded.

"The beauty expressed by your appearance is a reflection of your worthy experiences and accumulated values. For example, you would not be advancing to M2 after ten days if you did not meet or exceed the requirements of the parental commission. Having successfully raised three children as you did, and on a quarantined world, is a badge of honor and distinction here; also a contributing factor to your appearance, your personal beauty. The acquisition of spiritual values is another factor in the quality and quantity of material and morontial beauty."

"How far do you think we will be advanced?" Kala asked.

"I know not," replied Solonia. "Would you like to make an appointment with the counselors, the Evangels?"

"To plan our route to Edentia?" Saro asked.

"Yes," Solonia answered.

"When may we?" Kala asked.

"Tomorrow."

While waiting for the outdoor bistro to open, the trio sat watching the mix of beings as they strode by. Kala and Saro were feeling the cosmic vibrancy and spiritual energy of M1 ever stronger. Each day they were realizing more of the true joy of being and the richness of morontia life. They especially enjoyed watching angels interacting with other beings. And they were fascinated by the variety of languages and intonations they heard from passersby.

Each snippet of conversation was accompanied by the singing of birds and faint music drifting in from other venues.

After a while Saro said to Solonia, "We don't know the names of mansion food, only the unbelievably wonderful taste. What do you recommend?" Just then a transformation took place at the restaurant's center. An opening appeared in the ground and a group of servers with a full raft of prepared dishes and drinks rose from chambers concealed below. At once a server brought their guests chilled water in marvelously sculpted pitchers with matching drinking vessels.

Solonia said, "Until you are familiar with our foods, I can select for you." She placed their orders, then explained some of the menu icons to the pair so they would better know their name, type, and appearance. Already had they learned some of the symbols and pronunciation of the System language.

As they listened and learned more from Solonia, a large excursion pod landed with enough hungry beings to fill all the tables to overflowing. Kala and Saro seized the opportunity to invite a couple to share their table.

Solonia recognized their language on hearing them speak. She introduced the four. Kala and Saro were immediately impressed by their charm and obvious humility, as well as their curious language. Conversing through Solonia, they discovered that the couple are siblings, recently resurrected and now on liberty, from another of the System's spheres, Panoptia.

Kala instantly recalled and remarked, "That's the world saved from rebellion by the young leader, um...Ellanora! She kept your world from falling into the rebellion, and not one soul was lost — correct?" Solonia translated and their new friends replied affirmatively, adding that they are on the way to join their fellow Panoptians who are tarrying on the Father's sphere, Transition World Number Seven, care-taking and modifying that sacred place, doing it under Michael's orders and for an unknown future use.

After a friendly exchange of personal backgrounds, Solonia asked the Panoptians if they would like to send their menu selections to the service staff. She did so after they heard her recommendations.

While they waited, conversation ceased momentarily and they shared an experience of being absorbed in the moment amid the sights, sounds, and smells of this charming place. Every experience contributed to the discovery of deeper and deeper levels of the seventy senses with which morontia bodies are endowed. That sensory richness now manifested as gratitude, humility, joy, and divine insight.

The four thoroughly enjoyed the meal, thanking Solonia prodigiously for the selection. And they each acknowledged the dinner was made better by this chance meeting. The encounter with the Panoptians also made Saro and Kala curious about the history of all the System's 619 worlds, especially the other thirty-six that fell into rebellion with Urantia.

They also began to realize how fortunate they were in taking origin on Urantia, the 37th rebellion-seared world. The same world where Michael, the sovereign leader and co-creator of millions of architectural and evolutionary worlds, took up mortal life on his seventh and final bestowal, as the babe of Bethlehem, as Jesus the god-man of Urantia. And also where Nebadon's most recent rebellion was terminated. More than once had they heard the sentiment, 'You're Agondonters from Urantia. Lucky you!'

When the dinner was finished, the trio bade the Panoptian siblings farewell and Godspeed, then set off walking along the canal's bank. The night sky was speckled with stars near and far. Saro and Kala were becoming accustomed to their pattern. On the surface an endless parade of evening activities passed before their wonderfully sharp eyes, and entered their morontia hearing with its astonishing range and clarity.

The street musicians were plentiful and remarkably skilled. Some sang or played solo, but usually, two or more entertained the passing throngs. Some were playing instruments completely new to Saro and Kala. They created sounds and chord combinations Kala and Saro had never heard, or even imagined.

They had no doubt their senses, all of them, were improving, sharpening, broadening, and rapidly. What a joy to see and hear such marvelous and creative diversity. The entertainers and activities on this lovely boulevard created a symphony of background sound, filling their ears with the charming rhythms and tempos of mansion world life.

"Are there evening concerts on M1?" asked Saro.

"There are countless concerts, chorales, recitations, and improvs every night on M1 that music aficionados like you would surely enjoy. In fact, one is very close, and it happens to feature the work of a composer from Urantia, one you researched briefly at the registry. He is now a member of the Celestial Artisan Corps, and will conduct tonight's concert. You of course recall the classical composer, Handel?"

Kala said, "I do! In fact, we were part of an epic production of his Messiah. Remember, Saro? We were in London. It was an unforgettable experience."

"Yes, I recall," said Saro. "It was moving. Divinely so."

"There are a few seats still available, high in the gallery. Messiah is the feature, and this version he recently re-adapted for the morontia sound spectrum. I have experienced previous versions, and have anticipated hearing his newest with keen relish. How fortuitous he should be debuting his latest while you are here. Care to attend?"

"YES!!" said the pair in harmony.

On the way to the concert Solonia informed them, "The amphitheater holds 300,000." It was almost full when they walked in. The variety of beings in attendance was staggering. The musicians were already tuning their instruments. Even that cacophony revealed new ranges in their morontia hearing.

On the way to their seats they walked past the orchestra. The pair was riveted by the variety of instruments they saw, some recognizable, some quite elaborate and very strange in appearance. The "Great Harp" was indeed immense, "with seven thousand strings played by seventy Celestial Artisans," said Solonia.

They took their seats, high up on the theater's rim, and immediately felt at home luxuriating in the delightful concert atmosphere. Both were thinking of trying each of the mansion world instruments in the orchestra, and longing to play the morontia equivalent of their instruments of training with a group of celestial musicians.

Then proceeded a wondrous experience in sound, the complexity of which pervaded the depths of their being, and the soaring heights of which well complemented that morning's flight over M1. The live mixture of choral song and instrumental sound exceeded anything they had previously experienced. Saro and Kala were enjoying every note, chord, and strain, playing it on their respective instruments in their minds, where much music memory from their Urantia lives was now surfacing.

They left the concert so moved there was nothing to do but stop outside the exit gate and worship the God who created the potentials, possibilities, creators, administrators, and inspiration that produces such experience. They were not alone in worship, as a ring of humble and grateful beings, of many orders, formed in the spacious park grounds surrounding the amphitheater.

After a while, when a majority of the post-concert worshipers had departed, Solonia excused herself saying she would come at dawn and escort them to their counseling session with the Evangels. The trio enjoyed a loving embrace after which Solonia summoned a transport to her abode.

The pair stayed and indulged yet another urge to worship. They lay face-up on soft grass, becoming absorbed in the night sky. Their connection to the Divine Indwellers was improving significantly with each day's passing. Neither of them had felt such firm and continued connectedness with their Indwelling Paradise Partners as they now were.

It was past midnight before they called for a transport home. Viewing M1 at night from the air for the first time was a perfect ending to such a day. They embraced and kissed as they flew over a vast landscape of life and light, where never a body dies nor ages. Their satisfaction was supreme.

After landing at their lodge's front gate, the pair followed their now established pattern and walked through the adjacent park before retiring. They were feeling very much at peace within themselves, and more in love with God, life, and each other, than ever. And tomorrow they would discuss their immediate destiny with the Seraphic Evangels.

Saro remarked, "You know, as exciting as all of this is, what's going on inside is more so. I'm sensing the same happening with you, yes?"

"I was wondering about you too. You're feeling much closer to your Adjuster?"

"I am feeling more and more connected," replied Saro. "His messages are flashing directly into my mind, clear and dear. There is clarity and the sense that we are as one. And! I'm almost certain of sensing his rejoicing. You?"

"Yes. It's beautiful for all four of us...And it has a lot to do with this culture, its bent toward one purpose, one that aligns with our purpose. It's the unity without uniformity we always wanted and tried to create on Urantia — a spiritual environment that fosters progress in the inner and outer life at the same time."

"It feels right. Very right," said Saro. "What all's in the UB about the Evangels we're meeting in the morning." He accessed the related text.

"There are several mentions...Seraphic Evangels do more than one thing."

"As I recall, it was an Evangel who 'whispered to the shepherd boy,'" Kala said.

"It was. How many times did we read this prayer on Urantia?" Saro read it to her once more:

"The Gods are my caretakers; I shall not stray;

Side by side they lead me in the beautiful paths and glorious refreshing of life everlasting.

I shall not, in this Divine Presence, want for food nor thirst for water.

Though I go down into the valley of uncertainty or ascend up into the worlds of doubt,

Though I move in loneliness or with the fellows of my kind,

Though I triumph in the choirs of light or falter in the solitary places of the spheres,

Your good spirit shall minister to me, and your glorious angel will comfort me.

Though I descend into the depths of darkness and death itself, I shall not doubt you nor fear you,

For I know that in the fullness of time and the glory of your name

You will raise me up to sit with you on the battlements on high." (48:6.9)

After returning and retiring to their bed, Kala pondered, "What will the Evangels advise? Have you thought much about routes? I haven't."

"I haven't either. There's too much we don't know."

"Let's rest, my love, and think about it tomorrow." She caressed his face, he kissed hers tenderly.

~ Chapter 12 ~
Personal Religious Experience, The Evangels

Well before daybreak Kala and Saro exchanged massages, showered, dressed, and discovered a tall drink of fruit juice some unseen, solicitous servant had left on the swinging platform in back of their residence. They gave the swing a push, mounted it, then sat back to back at its center and enjoyed the juice, followed by a morning embrace with their Divine Indwellers. Night birds sang a light and charming melody as they sipped.

And as the swing ever so gradually came to a stop, so did their morontia minds. They became absorbed in the moment, completely aware of the outer world and at one with the inner. This happened to them simultaneously as they sat perfectly still in worshipful attitude. It was as if all four, two Adjusters and two ascending souls, were one in the moment. Suddenly all four of their Guardian Angels joined in this mutual experience of divine attunement and God-consciousness.

Saro's and Kala's minds held perfect peace as they viewed Adjuster picturizations of their Paradise destiny and the route to it. Then they beheld flashes of their Indweller's past lives, followed by details of their projected path to fusion. They were shown sights and signposts of cosmic history and universe progress that every Paradise ascender eventually witnesses. But they were seeing them here, now, and in rapid succession, like a language without words.

During this personal spiritual experience, they were given worlds of insight and vast quantities of information, most of which they were able to absorb with little or no difficulty. They were shown glimpses of countless cities of God that lie on every pilgrims' path, Jerusem, Edentia, Salvington, Uversa, Havona, even Paradise. They beheld astounding images that defy description, others that defied understanding but must have deep significance or relevance in their future. The pair did innately comprehend that many of the images they perceived were much about the spirit world and its activities, well beyond the simple quasi-physical terrain they were now traversing.

Lastly, they were permitted a vision of themselves at the moment of fusion with their Indwellers. They could feel the intense and unspoken love of God, Michael, Mother, and the angels, lifting them to divine heights of unlimited glory and light. This was a transcendent experience of cosmic insight about their future, as well as confirmation of divine approval of performance during their rugged test on Urantia.

Finally, Saro and Kala lost track of time and space, suspended in the embrace of God and his angels. They were made aware that some of the things witnessed during this revelatory experience had to be stored for future reference. There were some revelations and insights beyond their present capacity to grasp, things that must await the development of greater conceptual scaffolding.

Never would the pair forget this moment of inner and outer contact on their fourth morning as morontians. Daylight was well in evidence when the pair descended from the heavenly heights of timeless/spaceless divine insight and transcendent worship. They sat for a while simply being, breathing ever so slowly, feeling at one with eyes shut, at the same time seeing all things in a new light.

No outer experience could match the beauty, goodness and truth of this inner experience with God, Michael, the Divine Minister, along with their attending angels. Saro and Kala were both realizing this experience, with its many pictures of destiny, would help them decide on the choices the Seraphic Evangels will put before them this very morning.

Before they had a chance to discuss this mutual revelatory

experience, their Guardians departed and Solonia arrived. She greeted them with great warmth, noting a new and finer light coming from the pair. She remarked, "My, but you are learning quickly."

On their walk to the Seraphic Evangels' meeting, located at another of the edifices within the immense Resurrection Hall complex, the trio talked about Kala's and Saro's insight-filled experience.

"It was an experience of wonder. I was perfectly aware that Saro and I were having the same experience," Kala said.

"Me too! It was as if all eight of us were of one mind. It was truly wonderful, and enlightening," said Saro. "Do all your wards have this kind of experience?"

Solonia counseled them saying, "Such experiences have occurred, but they are not the norm. I estimate the near perfect alignment of your closely kindred minds, resonant souls, matched purpose, and harmonized personalities are unusual but fortuitous. Perhaps that facilitated your apparently identical experiences — although I would caution against such an assumption.

"Also, simply being on this world is a powerful stimulus for spiritual experience and quick growth, especially at first. And doubt not that your Guardians are working for you on unseen levels, even as one or both of them always watches over you. I expect they will draw close to you once again at this morning's meeting, as well as your Monitors, who are intensely interested in the career decisions and spiritual welfare of their betrothed."

Solonia departed when they arrived at the Evangel's quarters, agreeing to rejoin them after the meeting. The Evangels' offices are as beautiful as any they had seen. It too is roofless, and overlaid with a multitude of lustrous metals, punctuated by a wide variety of stunning gems, all arranged in aesthetically appealing patterns, shapes and forms. Everything is accented with flowering vines and lush plants. The Evangels themselves could not have been more charming, solicitous, or desirous of serving them.

After their greeting and name exchange, the lead Evangel offered them seats and asked, in Saro and Kala's language, "You are aware of our order of being and our domains of service?"

Kala answered, "You are sixth order seraphic servers, all daughters of the Divine Minister. In *The Urantia Book* you're called 'Transition Ministers.' Saro and I re-read the statements about your order last night, about your work as counselors. And all Urantia has heard the beautiful prayer whispered to the shepherd boy by an Evangel. Was that one of you?"

They laughed. It was the first time Saro and Kala had heard angel laughter. The beauty of its sound stirred their souls to love angels even more.

"No. We laugh because we were with her only yesterday. In fact she asked us to send you greetings and congratulations. We, all three, have served on Urantia. And like most beings in Nebadon we are always interested in news from Urantia. Not only because it is the world of Michael's seventh bestowal, also because the new revelation by book has been seeded and germinated there. In fact, you two are the first couple to simultaneously ascend to Mansonia after the third day on the wings of new revelation."

Saro replied, "Our Guardians..." Suddenly all four Guardians appeared behind the pair. Saro paused and smiled at them, then continued, "Our guardians said we will go on to M2 after ten days. May we know how long we will be on M2? How far are we to progress before taking up residence?"

The spokesperson for the Evangels drew closer, speaking in mellifluous tones, "Saro, Kala, being the first pilgrim couple to arrive on Mansonia by simultaneously embracing and sincerely following the teachings of Urantia's latest revelation, and being two so very well adjusted and service minded, we the Seraphic Evangels — with the advice and consent from your Adjusters and your Guardians — have created a plan for your mansion world transition. It is the considered opinion of everyone involved — and approved by the Counsel of twenty-four Elders on Jerusem — that you be advanced every ten days to M7."

Kala's and Saro's eyes widened as the Evangel continued; they were too surprised to speak. "Of course we have provided for your rejection of our plan. There are other paths that might also meet with acceptance by the System administrators. You may wish to ask that modifications be made to any course." She paused, then added, "You should not be surprised. We aren't. We reviewed your life records, conferred with your Guardians, sought the advice of all concerned, and concluded you two are excellent subjects for a special service."

She paused again to allow the pair to steady their composure. After the morning's intimate experience with their Adjusters and Guardians, a bit of themselves was still in that experience. The pictures of their destinies and their Adjusters' previous indwellings continued to echo in their minds. In fact, given the visions they received that morning, the climb to M7 now appeared relatively modest in comparison to the rest of the journey to God, it being merely the first rung on the ladder to the Paradise abode.

The Evangel went on to say, "Saro, Kala, the transcripts of your lives reflect an ideal model of what we are all hoping to see come from *The Urantia Book* experiment. All eyes are on the integration and repercussions of the new text revelation to the flagship world of Nebadon. It is already bearing good fruit. You are living evidence of its efficacy.

"During your lives you steered a course that exemplified wise choices at almost every turn. Your early discovery of, and reliance on, your Adjuster's wisdom impressed your angels. This affected every aspect of your lives, particularly your parenting. While on Urantia, and in spite of all the hazards of living on a quarantined world — even though you often dealt with multiple and simultaneous pressures — you very successfully raised three children. All of whom we anticipate will someday arrive here. They in turn are raising others in your parenting tradition."

One of Kala's Guardians reminded them of Andon's humorous remark to Kala and Saro at Banquet Hall, "'...the number of your seed may someday match mine and Fonta's.' That could hardly be so, given Andon and Fonta's million year head start, but you should not miss Andon's point about the magnitude of your positive effect on Urantia's unique history and population, the great social value derived from your experience and instruction, your lasting influence on Urantia."

The Evangel continued, "The parental commissioners have approved your quick passage across Mansonia, as have we. Not only are you paragons of parenting, your ceaseless seeking advice in prayer, and your finding the divine embrace in worship indicated to us, and well before you died, the harmonious functioning of all seven adjutants. And again, this morning, you registered on the highest levels of spirit consciousness of which you are capable.

"Your angels have observed in you a willingness always to put the welfare of others before your own. You have consistently displayed loyalty and wisdom in your choices. You have habitually sought out the divine will and done all in your power to execute it. We find little trace of the 'mark of the beast' in you. Indeed, you showed moderation in all things except worship.

"In all your dealings as adults on Urantia, neither of you showed a shade of selfishness or dishonesty. When problems larger than yourselves were forced upon you, you always went to the inner bastion for advice and the restorative, harmonizing effects of worship, ever relying on the divine. We who have been to Urantia and know of its many problems and great potentials do salute the progress of those who have embraced revelation, died, ascended, and stand here ready to serve."

Saro and Kala were elated to receive these words of approval from such brilliant and experienced angelic administrators. They had indeed been tireless toilers for the establishment of the kingdom of God in the hearts of women and men of Urantia. They had certainly earned what is being offered.

The lead Evangel spoke again saying, "I mentioned a special service. On occasion certain groups are formed that help accelerate our plans for mortal ascension from resurrection to fusion. We see you as excellent choices to found and lead such a group. We are asking if you will consider joining other highly successful individuals who, like you, showed extraordinary progress in mortal life, relying wholly on faith, angels, Indwellers, and of course, each other.

"Our aim is to create an ever-growing core of mortal survivors, ones who have fused, have consummated a union with their Adjusters and who will volunteer to return to M2 to help teach and lead an exceptionally large resurrection class that will be coming up from Urantia after the next dispensational resurrection."

Immediately Kala and Saro asked at the same time, "When will that be?"

There was a shared and growing affection within this little group, one of spiritual harmony and profound mutual respect. Kala and Saro thought about the variety of beings these Evangels must surely counsel in their everyday work as Mansonian ministers. The pair was also feeling very close to their Adjusters at this moment of decision, as the morning's revelatory experience again resonated in their supple, expanding, morontia minds.

"Before we go further, you should know that you may, if you so decide, extend the ten days of liberty on any of the mansion worlds by ten day increments. There is room for flexibility in your itinerary. Our projected goal is to have your special mission group assembled, fully trained, and ready for service in 300 System years."

"That's about three hundred Urantia years." Saro

estimated.

The Evangel replied, "Yes...minus 19.1 percent. We believe Urantia's next dispensational resurrection is imminent, perhaps in fewer than one thousand planetary years. Of course Michael could return to Urantia today and trigger the next mass resurrection. We do not know. We do know the current dispensation will end before long. Then hundreds of millions of sleeping Urantians will resurrect here on M1, in every imaginable psychological condition, and speaking many languages, several of which you are already familiar. But each resurrectee will have at least a flicker of faith and an abiding hunger for truth. They will want to learn the facts and hear the truths you already know and have lived.

"Before they arrive you should have time enough to ascend Mansonia, fuse, and return to establish and implement a training program that will prepare your team for the coming wave of Urantians. Your special mission group will be under the direct supervision of Andon and Fonta, and it will be headquartered with the Mansion World Teachers.

"As we anticipate Mansonia's future needs — that is another area of Seraphic Evangel responsibility — we have deemed it wise to establish this group of ex-mortals who have transitioned up the mansion world regime, fused with their Monitors, and volunteered to return and lead a large class of resurrected pilgrims over the same path. Even more importantly, you will be living proof that it can be done, and that the effort is well worth it.

"This means that you will forfeit the experience of looking into Mansonia's every aspect, facility, and temple — for the time being. But you will have ample time as you move up Mansonia as fused beings along with your assigned class. Groups, naturally, move more slowly than individuals. Indeed, no class may advance en masse until its slowest members advance. Of course, after fusion, you and your team of leaders will be free to use every service on any world of the System to prepare yourselves to help lead this future class from Urantia."

"How many others have you selected for this group?" Kala asked.

"You are the first. As the founding members, you will be its leaders and spokespersons, under Andon and Fonta's guidance of course. At this point I will mention that your Guardians informed me you both were certified as having achieved the second psychic circle, after your Adjuster communion this morning. This indicates your use of mota in combination with worship has already replaced the need for the scaffolding of faith."

They took a moment. Saro and Kala were not in the least anxious about being confronted with this decision. Still, they both wanted to discuss each route and course option they might take, together or apart. The Evangels then proceeded to put all the possibilities and options before them.

Kala and Saro truly loved each other with an equal and ever growing affection, and did not wish to separate. By the Evangel's proffered plan they could remain together for the mansion world phase of their ascension. That could be a long while if they are to accompany and guide a great class of pilgrims up and through the mansion training regime. And why not see the mansion worlds as fused beings? Would not then their perspective be greater, and they be better able to see what is truly meaningful, valuable, and of good purpose, and thereby know even greater ways to be of service?

The meeting adjourned with the Evangels retiring, leaving the pair, their four Guardians and two Adjusters, to meditate on the Seraphic Evangels' counsel. And that they did.

After a short period of silent and sincere prayer, and with assurance from her Adjuster, Kala looked straight into Saro's eyes and said, "If I know you as well as I think I do, you already know there is only one choice."

Saro had sensed the same assurance and answered, "If I know you as well as I think I do, then the choice is already made."

~ Chapter 13 ~
Touring M1

With all four Guardians and their Adjusters as witnesses, Kala and Saro then and there decided to take the Evangel's recommended route. Their Guardians congratulated them roundly and warmly. Then one of Saro's angels asked, "Now, will you change your plans for the remainder of your stay on M1?"

They thought a moment after which Kala asked Saro, "Why don't we spend the rest of the day thinking over our short-term plans, now that we've all agreed on the long term?"

Saro took her arm saying, "Let's do."

At that point their Guardians embraced them and vanished. Kala and Saro left the Evangels' circle on foot. They wandered without direction thinking over the day's unexpected events, at the same time enjoying the sights and sounds of the beautiful living tableau that is the resurrection complex.

When the pair walked by Banquet Hall's garden, they decided to enter. Being so close to the luxuriant, cultivated shrubs and plants, laden with a wide variety of fruit, colorful vegetables and aromatic herbs, induced them to sniff, sample, and share. They recognized several varieties, having enjoyed their taste at the banquet. They tried different items; the riper ones were rich and unbelievably delicious.

They sat down in a tiny lattice-work chapel at the end of a long row of tall viney, flowering plants with large clusters of delectable, multi-colored fruit. The chapel nook was made of a morontia material they had not seen before. Saro described it as "soft crystal." They relaxed there, taking in the beauty of the garden and watching the spornagia tend the plants.

"Just one circle to go, eh?" Saro said with a tone of amazement.

"Apparently!" exclaimed Kala. "I do feel, more or less, in constant contact ever since this morning. You too?"

"I do. And during our experience I got the impression my Partner wanted me to take the Evangels' offer," said Saro. "But I didn't really get that until we were in the Evangel's meeting."

"Same for me. You and I are so alike in mind and spirit. And now I've realized, we're a foursome." Kala embraced the air as if hugging her Paradise Partner. "They're in and with us, and now we're more conscious of them, and on a higher level. It's like a dream of heaven coming true. It's as if I'm floating on a river of joy, spirit joy like I've never known. We're in heaven already Saro, and if we're feeling this way on M1, what will we feel, know, and be, by the time we reach M7?! Anyway, I'm sure my Partner knows I was surprised to hear we have permission to advance all the way to M7, skipping along every ten days. And I'm sure I felt his joy when we agreed to the Evangel's plan. It made me think of that line, what was it exactly?"

She located the text, "It's from a Solitary Messenger: *'The Adjuster, while passive regarding purely temporal welfare, is divinely active concerning all the affairs of your eternal future.'*" (110:1.4)

After a moment Saro replied, "The Evangel said we could have additional ten-day liberties on any mansion world. I like that part. She didn't say this, but it was implied that somewhere between here and M7, we'll make the 1st psychic circle. Then we do whatever else is required before fusing, on the upper mansions, presumably...and yes my love, I've had an increased sense of shared joy since this morning. I feel so loved, and I do so love. I keep hearing in my mind, and feeling, the simplest and most profound of all truths: 'God is love.'"

The fruits they ate only piqued their appetites. After a short while they decided to walk to an eatery outside the Resurrection Hall complex, taking a different gate this time. As they ambled along unknown avenues Kala said, "We have eight days left on M1. What should we do, ask for ten additional days? Spend them the way we originally planned; visiting the temple of Morontia Companions, the governor's residence, tour the surface? Do you still want to certify for bird piloting?"

"I don't sense any indication of problems with our original plan, do you?"

"No. I was just thinking about how to use the liberties, now that we know our route and the approximate time frame. Unless we opt to extend on one of the mansions, we have sixty-eight days of liberty left, total...Which would be about six months on Urantia."

Saro pondered the situation and said, "In a way, this is a pre-honeymoon trip up the mansion worlds. This is our final period of betrothal. I keep seeing the finality of it, to be secure in eternity always seemed like a far, far away goal. Until now.

"And those images of our destiny expanded my vision of eternity in ways I can't even begin to verbalize. But I can see clearly, so much of the past and some of the future."

"We are indeed fortunate," said Saro with deep sincerity, selfless humility, and genuine gratitude.

For the remainder of their days on M1, one by one, Kala and Saro ticked off places to go and things to do. Each day's activity was interspersed with worship, rest, and play. During this short period of liberty they spoke with scores of residents and guests, many of whom were able to give the pair insights and guidance. They in turn did good as they passed by, just as was their habit on Urantia.

While on M1 the pair gained an idea of the scope of the training the sphere offers. With regard to resurrected ascenders, it was apparent that the better part of it pertains to deficiency ministry. They attained a sense of correctness of the text Kala recalled from *The Urantia Book*'s revelations about M1: *"Survivors arriving on this first of the detention spheres present so many and such varied defects of creature character and deficiencies of mortal experience that the major activities of the realm are occupied with the correction and cure of these manifold legacies of the life in the flesh."* (47:3.8)

They also toured the factory where the harps of God are manufactured. Kala and Saro were astounded on seeing the techniques employed by the workers, and the efficiency of the manufacturing process. At the factory they met and talked with a variety of beings in both management and production. Almost all were interested in their stories of life on Urantia.

On another occasion they returned to the great bird house in the sky for piloting lessons. This took all morning of one day, and that afternoon the pair made a long round-trip flight to the renowned Morontia Companions' temple. They toured the area briefly then enjoyed a memorable worship session amid several million other beings of highly diverse orders.

They also took an afternoon for a field study of the immense variety of lower life forms of M1, the plants and animals. The diversity, uniqueness, and fearlessness of the morontia creatures immediately impressed them. They enjoyed the easy and gentle interspecies contact with a fascinating spectrum of wildlife, and concluded without a doubt that an absence of fear between creatures is normal here. No creature has to devour another to survive.

One day they spent traveling to and touring M1 headquarters. There they took a guided tour of the governor's residence and its magnificent hanging garden. From one of the gardens' promenades Saro and Kala watched in complete fascination as seraphic transporters took off and landed on a far-away high point; The site where they would soon depart M1 for M2.

It was on M1 that the pair encountered a group of High Commissioners, Spirit-fused beings. Spirit-fusers are not Adjustered, they are destined to serve in the local universe. Most never ascend to Paradise. Saro recalled reading about these kindred beings who, like them, took origin on the evolutionary planets.

"After attaining the Nebadon Corps of Perfection, Spirit-

fused ascenders may accept assignment as Universe Aids, this being one of the avenues of continuing experiential growth which is open to them. Thus do they become candidates for commissions to the high service of interpreting the viewpoints of the evolving creatures of the material worlds to the celestial authorities of the local universe." (37:5.4)

Kala asked, "Solonia, Spirit-fusers attain perfection only at the local level, correct?"

"Yes, that's correct. They have a home world; the eighth major sphere in the Salvington circuit. You will be invited to visit them after you pass through the Edentia schools and arrive at Nebadon's capital. I have many Spirit-fused friends. They, like me, are permanent residents of the local universe. They know it like no transient being ever could. And there are over a billion and a half "High Commissioners" in all Nebadon."

Each night they returned to their lodging in the Melchizedek sector. Each day they sampled the sights, sounds, scents, and tastes of several different locales. The connecting link to all this movement and experience was their constant and affirmative response to the worship urge. In temple after temple they strengthened bonds with their beloved Indwellers by the power and creativity of inner communion.

The eight days passed quickly, but the pair did pick up much valuable experience and a new sense of belonging to life at the morontia level. Life takes on new and unimagined meaning, value, and purpose as pilgrims ascend in spirit. Still, there was a great deal of M1 that had to be left unexplored until they returned.

The night before departing M1, Solonia made arrangements for seraphic transport to M2. Kala and Saro spent their last evening at Banquet Hall, dining with some of the friends they had made during their M1 stay. Solonia was with them. At the end of the meal the trio talked about the transport process; seraphic sleep, and reawakening on another world.

"Do you self-transport, or travel like us, by Seraphim?"

Saro asked Solonia.

"We leave that to the specialists — Transport Seraphim. Shall we meet at your abode at dawn and take a transport to the launch?"

They agreed and Kala said, "Solonia, we talked it over and want to request that you accompany us to M7. If you want to, we would be honored by your company." Saro nodded agreement.

"As a matter of fact, just this morning, my request to remain with you, as long as you want, was approved. I was about to mention it." They cheered and embraced. Their first solid, personal, inter-species friendship on Mansonia was with a Morontia Companion, a daughter of the Divine Minister, one who will be welcoming and escorting beings like Saro and Kala up and down the System's worlds until Light and Life permeates all Nebadon.

From the Banquet Hall the trio headed to the Melchizedek sector, discussing the eventful day as they strolled. Solonia remarked on their equanimity, maturity, and sagacity throughout the day. She also congratulated the pair on taking up the challenge put before them by the Evangels. She then asked to be excused for the night. The three shared an especially warm and lingering embrace.

Kala and Saro did not feel the need to rest. Both were energized and living in sweet and profound awareness of their Adjusters, stimulated significantly by more reflections on the day's inner and outer revelations. They decided to return to the gazebo at the center of the park where their first night on M1 was spent. They climbed to the top tier and looked out over the lighted sphere, drinking in the wonder and beauty of it.

After a long period of silence, Kala said, "Our first time to enseraphim, Saro, tomorrow! Too bad we won't be awake for it."

"We shouldn't sleep for long. M2 is close. At three times light speed, it can't take long."

They settled in for a night of quiet talks, intimate personal association, and divine communion, interspersed with occasional walks. Their Adjusters continued to flash picturizations of previous indwellings. Kala and Saro exchanged stories they had just witnessed, and noted the values wrought from lives that did not resurrect. Their Indwellers revealed many, many experiences that gave the pair undreamed-of insight into the trials and failures of those other beings. Indeed, Kala and Saro felt as if they were gathering insight into cosmic existence itself.

Solonia found the pair still at the gazebo the next morning. She climbed up and sat with them. The trio discussed their departure, then returned to their lodging for freshening up and a change of wrap.

During the ride to the site of seraphic transportation, Saro reviewed the Urantia text about their impending enseraphiming and read it aloud at Kala's request:

"When enseraphimed, you go to sleep for a specified time, and you will awake at the designated moment. The length of a journey when in transit sleep is immaterial. You are not directly aware of the passing of time. It is as if you went to sleep on a transport vehicle in one city and, after resting in peaceful slumber all night, awakened in another and distant metropolis. You journeyed while you slumbered. And so you take flight through space, enseraphimed, while you rest — sleep. The transit sleep is induced by the liaison between the Adjusters and the seraphic transporters." (39:2.12)

"Have you read *The Urantia Book*, Solonia?" asked Kala.

"I have, more than once. We all relished reports from Urantia about progress during the book's inception, and finally its publication. *The Urantia Book* is the most popular of all Mansonia literature. Part IV has been transformed into a day-long production. Every Mansonian eventually witnesses it many times, and in many versions. The Celestial Artisans are always working on improving their presentations of the greatest story ever to unfold in Nebadon."

"This is what we so longed for on Urantia! And it lasts an entire M1 day?!" Saro asked.

Big smiles broke out on their faces. They looked at each other and Saro said, "Do we need reservations?"

"Never. There are always multiple versions running on each of the seven mansions. And of course you may view a recording privately, at your lodging, via your harp. But I recommend you set aside a day on M2 to see it performed live."

"Let's do that!" Kala said gleefully. They were very happy to discover this. Kala and Saro had often talked about the impact of the creation of a series of movies based on the Midwayers' account of the Master's life as it is portrayed in Part IV, in order that all the world might have access to it. Now they could see it, and not in three or four short Urantia hours, but over a whole mansion world day. They were pleased to know another of their fondest wishes would soon be fulfilled, even if not on Urantia.

Saro then uttered a prophesy, "Someday Urantia will have passenger birds again, and first rate depictions of Michael's incarnation as Jesus."

~ Chapter 14 ~
Seraphic Transport, Arriving on M2

M1's seraphic transport point is a modest mount located not far from its headquarters, also the energy pole of the sphere. Kala and Saro had viewed this mount of angelic departure and arrival in fascination just days before from the governor's promenade where they were touring.

Solonia instructed the pod to approach slowly so the pair had time to watch the landing and launching of several beings at close range. She told them, "The M1 spaceport is surrounded by receiving stations for visiting beings of diverse orders." Pointing to a ring of structures around the top of the mount she said, "That zone is where we register. And there is the make-ready area, where seraphic sleep is induced."

The pair watched the center of the surface of a large glassy field on the mount's top as Seraphim in one area — along with several assistants — enshrouded their living, sleeping cargo and launched. One shot off almost immediately after another. In an adjacent area just as many Seraphim were landing, opening their shields, awakening their passengers, and moving off the field. The process flowed without ceasing; a stunning and beautiful two-way parade of beings and light.

As soon as they landed, a Companion greeted them, "You are Kala and Saro Maylon, due to transport to M2 this morning?" Solonia presented their authorization for seraphic travel which the Companion certified and recorded. Solonia then led them to the sleep induction station just off the launch zone where all three were made ready for seraphic slumber and transport.

"This is your first seraphic ride," remarked the chief of

transport in good English. "You are taking Solonia too! How fortunate for you," she smiled at Solonia.

"We are old, old friends," Solonia said, adding, "I will return, and with Kala and Saro."

"Special mission?" the transport chief asked.

"Yes. Escorting these two prodigies to M7." Solonia answered.

"Ready?" All three nodded.

"See you on another world, my love," said Kala.

"Until then," replied Saro.

The Companion had them each lie on long soft tables that floated waist high off the surface. After lying on it and closing eyes, the transit sleep hit and they were awake no more.

The night before their first enseraphiming Kala and Saro reviewed the revelations about the physical and visual aspects of an angelic launch. Kala read it:

"When celestial beings are to be enseraphimed for transfer from one world to another, they are brought to the headquarters of the sphere and, after due registry, are inducted into the transit sleep. Meantime, the transport seraphim moves into a horizontal position immediately above the universe energy pole of the planet. While the energy shields are wide open, the sleeping personality is skillfully deposited, by the officiating seraphic assistants, directly on top of the transport angel. Then both the upper and lower pairs of shields are carefully closed and adjusted. And now, a strange metamorphosis begins as the seraphim is made ready to swing into the energy currents of the universe circuits. To outward appearance the seraphim grows pointed at both extremities and becomes so enshrouded in an odd light of amber hue that very soon it is impossible to distinguish the enseraphimed personality. When all is in readiness for departure, the chief of transport makes the proper inspection of the carriage of life, carries out the routine tests to ascertain whether or not the angel is properly encircuited, and then announces that the

traveler is properly enseraphimed, that the energies are adjusted, that the angel is insulated, and that everything is in readiness for the departing flash. The mechanical controllers, two of them, next take their positions. By this time the transport seraphim has become an almost transparent, vibrating, torpedo-shaped outline of glistening luminosity. Now the transport dispatcher of the realm summons the auxiliary batteries of the living energy transmitters, usually one thousand in number; as he announces the destination of the transport, he reaches out and touches the near point of the seraphic carriage, which shoots forward with lightning-like speed, leaving a trail of celestial luminosity as far as the planetary atmospheric investment extends." (39:5.14)

The next thing the trio saw was each other, awakening on M2's "sea of glass," surrounded by transport personnel. After awakening, Solonia, Kala, and Saro were led off the sea of glass to the reception area. The pair noted the design of the M2 seraphic transport hub is like M1's, but much larger and more elaborate.

They immediately shook off the seraphic sleep. The pair was in fact invigorated. But Solonia didn't seem affected in the least, enseraphiming being a routine procedure for her.

Saro said, "You must've done this a trillion times. Is it always the same? I don't remember a thing. Lying down is my last memory. Then we were here."

Solonia replied, "Always. It's as if no time passed for the transportee."

Kala looked around, "I recall reading M2 is the first mansion world with a sea of glass. It's gigantic, isn't it? And so busy!"

As seraphic transports landed and launched one after another, the rhythm and beauty of it mesmerized them. They could not stop watching this captivating scene of an ordinary mansion world spaceport in full service. They took a long moment to adjust to the fact that they were on the shores of a second world, and only sixteen days since they had died on

Urantia. And already, Urantia was a quickly fading reality, like old scaffolding.

Solonia informed Kala and Saro that she had just received a request to report for the first of their eight morontia adjustments. The pair had forgotten about this procedure in the flurry of excitement and activity on M1.

Solonia called for transportation to the temple with seventy radiating wings. It has chambers of transition similar to Resurrection Hall's. They registered and were escorted to a chamber where the procedure is implemented.

The technician joked with them, and in their tongue, "Greetings Urantia pilgrims. Ready to rev up your mota? Park it right here, please." They sat in high-backed seats that gently caressed them, and induced a pleasurable tingling.

"Will this hurt?" Kala asked.

"Are you hurting now?" the technician replied with a gentle smile. "Besides, what do Agony-donters care about hurt? You are Agony-donters, aren't you?" They had a big laugh at her malaprop. She then confessed that her last Urantian Anglophone "victim" gave her those jokes.

Solonia introduced them. "This is a sister of mine. We share the same source, the Mother of Nebadon. But she is one I have not met before. I do recognize her as a System Co-ordinator, one of seven varieties of Morontia Power Supervisors."

"Odd title for a body/mind surgeon," remarked Saro in kindly jest.

"Who issues these names, anyway?" she retorted. "I have renamed my job. I am a 'Morontia Body/Mind Beautification and Extenuation Technician, First Class.'"

"Then beautify and extend me," replied Saro.

"All right, coming up, one beautification and extension for the man from Urantia." Next the technician made their chairs recline and instructed them to relax, remain still, and ignore what was about to happen. Solonia observed as the multi-faceted, morontia energy mechanism hovered around each of them and silently did its work with the System Co-ordinator in close attendance, observing and controlling the process.

"Done. Just seven more between here and M7."

"That didn't take long. Should I feel different?" asked Saro.

"Give it seven days," the Co-ordinator advised, "and don't be afraid to rev up your mota." They departed with an embrace and smiles on their new morontia faces.

"Do I look different, Kala?"

"No, do I?"

Solonia said, "To me, you have the same form, the same soul, personality, and Adjuster, but your bodies and minds have been altered. And you will note, in seven days, that the mechanism of personality has been adjusted from your present state." She then recited a line often used to instruct ascenders about the adjustments: *'The progressive changes result in altered reactions to the morontia environment, such as modifications in food requirements and numerous other personal practices.'* " (48:2.23)

As they exited, Kala thought of their six relatives living and working on M2. "We should contact my parents, Joy, Will and your cousins," said Kala.

Saro added, "Hope they will be interested in viewing the M2 presentation of Jesus' life. We could attend a showing together. But I should have contacted Will and my cousins before we left M1."

"And I should have sent word to my parents," lamented Kala.

Solonia instantly felt she had failed them, "I let you down. I should apologize," she replied, almost tearfully. "A good host anticipates."

"You are good. And you don't need to apologize. We didn't tell you about our family members on M2," Kala assured her.

They both asked her forgiveness for making thoughtless statements. The pair embraced her and all three had a laugh over the incident. They were beginning to treasure the depth of sensitivity and desire to please that Solonia had shown ever since their first meeting in back of their residence on M1.

Solonia recommended they take a transport to Saro and Kala's assigned residence, first to settle in, then to contact their six relatives living and serving on M2. They agreed. The flight there allowed time for Solonia to give them information about the second mansion world, "This is what we recite to ascender's excursion groups coming up from M1 during their liberty:

"*It is on this sphere that you are more fully inducted into the mansonia life. The groupings of the morontia life begin to take form; working groups and social organizations start to function, communities take on formal proportions, and the advancing mortals inaugurate new social orders and governmental arrangements.* (47:4.1)

"*As you ascend the mansion worlds one by one, they become more crowded with the morontia activities of advancing survivors. As you go forward, you will recognize more and more of the Jerusem features added to the mansion worlds. The sea of glass makes its appearance on the second mansonia.* (47:4.3)

"*Mansonia number one is a very material sphere, presenting the early beginnings of the morontia regime. You are still a near human and not far removed from the limited viewpoints of mortal life, but each world discloses definite progress. From sphere to sphere you grow less material, more intellectual, and slightly more spiritual. The spiritual progress is greatest on the last three of these seven progressive worlds.* (47:4.6)

"*Mansonia number two more specifically provides for the removal of all phases of intellectual conflict and for the cure of all varieties of mental disharmony. The effort to master the significance of morontia mota, begun on the first mansion world, is here more earnestly continued. The development on mansonia number two compares with the intellectual status of the post-Magisterial Son culture of the ideal evolutionary worlds."* (47:4.8)

"That sounds very much like Urantia Book text," Saro said.

"I thought you might recognize it. In fact, we were honored when we learned the book's editors decided to include it in their mansion world descriptions. A staff member of the Brilliant Evening Star who authored Paper 47 heard it and asked permission to submit it to the editors for inclusion."

Their first aerial view confirmed there is a higher level of development on M2. It was obvious in the grander architecture and the increased scale of artistry. Even the artistic embellishments of their transport pod revealed a higher form of art. Kala and Saro could sense the change in culture. And perhaps, they thought, their recent adjustment was already taking effect.

"Solonia, you've been to all the worlds in the System, haven't you?" Saro asked.

"On many occasions. Eternal life affords us time to explore not only the System, but all Nebadon."

Kala then asked, "Do you sometimes wish to go outside Nebadon, even to Paradise?"

"Nebadon is my permanent home. I was designed for this place and this work. Stationary workers are needed to assist you ascenders. And one role is no more or less important than any other. Besides, my paradise is Salvington. That said, one can never know what the eternal ages will bring. I might be permitted to visit Paradise after light and life overtakes time and space."

"Have you been in the personal presence of Michael?" asked Saro.

"I have. Many times. And so shall you, soon enough."

When the pair had looked around their newest abode and

relaxed a bit, Solonia said, "Do you want to contact your family members while I file our authorizations? And I want also to make an appearance at my temporary residence."

Saro asked, "Where will you stay?"

"With an old friend who is serving on M2. He is a Life Carriers' assistant, one who helps with mass morontia resurrections — like yours. We've been friends for millennia, but haven't seen each other in a long while."

Kala said, "We'll contact Will, my parents and the others, Solonia. Go, check in at your friend's place. We'll be fine, and we'll contact you after we've spoken with our kinfolks."

Their new residence had a large pond not far from its back entrance. After a walk around it, observing the bountiful beauty of plant and animal life, they launched themselves in a small, highly polished metal rowboat that was among others moored to a pier extending out into the pond.

It was obvious the fauna and flora of M2 had an intricacy and beauty that was a step up from M1's. The appeal and complexity of M2's artistry took on new dimensions as did their physical senses. At the same time sensitivity to spirit leading was increasing, divine attunement was also waxing. That prompted Kala and Saro to realize that each step up the mansion world regime would probably bring unimagined, unprecedented uplift in every arena of being, from the lowest physical to the highest spiritual.

"Why don't we try to arrange a conference call among Will, Joy, my Mom and Dad, Joy, your cousins, and us?" asked Kala as she stopped rowing and let the boat go adrift.

Saro used his harp in an attempt to make a connection between all parties. But only Will was available.

"Welcome to M2, pilgrims!" said Will as his image appeared before them in full size. He appeared so real they reached out to touch him.

"Don't, that tickles." They laughed. "What's the matter,

didn't you like M1? Or you got the bums' rush already? You were always in trouble," Will joked.

"We didn't think we would be here so soon either. We want to tell you about it. But we'd like to tell you and the rest of the family in person and together. Can you break away for a day or two? We also want to view Jesus' life story with you and our other kin stationed here," Saro answered.

"How long will you be on M2?" Will asked.

"Only ten days," Kala said.

"Ten days only?! Yes, I can get away, especially if it is to see my favorite brother, and the beautiful mother of my nieces and nephew."

~ Chapter 15 ~
Family Visits, Jesus' Life Presentation

After connecting with Will, and before the morning was gone, the pair had contacted each of their other relatives. By shifting schedules and mutual agreement the group chose the seventh of Kala's and Saro's ten-day liberty on M2 to view a collaborative creation of the Reversion Directors and the Celestial Artisans, their highly-praised, day-long documentary presentation of the life and teachings of Jesus.

The eighth day they planned to spend in retreat, in celebration of being a member of Michael's universe family. The eighth day will also be a day of saying, "So long!" to their relatives, until they cross paths again as fused beings. Then Kala and Saro will be leading a class of ascending Agondonters on their way up from their world of mutual origin — tiny, remote, benighted Urantia.

The pair then contacted Solonia to give her their seventh and eighth day plan. She was pleased they could arrange the family meeting on such short notice, and asked, "What would you like to do and see the other days?"

Kala thought a moment and suggested, "Solonia, why don't you spend the rest of today as you like, and we'll use it to explore, discuss, and decide what all else to do while on M2? We will contact you as soon as we've decided." Saro nodded agreement.

"My friend and I have much we can do. So I will leave you to enjoy the rest of the day exploring, and wish you good night. And I will most certainly arrive at your lodging at first light tomorrow. I love you."

"And we you," they replied in unison.

Kala reflected happily on the quality of their deepening friendship with Solonia, "We're lucky to have her as a companion.

"Saro, what do you think we should do with our remaining days?"

"Our pilots' licenses are good all the way to M7, right?"

She smiled. "This afternoon?"

"Best way to see God's mansions!" declared Saro.

Until the seventh day of their stay the pair used their temporary residence as a base to make treks all over M2. They traveled much farther than on M1, and consequently spent considerable time in one form of transportation or another. They used part of this time to go within, to commune with their Indwellers. Some of this time they used to view the endlessly fascinating scenery while listening to Solonia's detailed information and historical facts about it. The pair also made time to interact with as many others as they could who were either living or sojourning on M2, of which there is a greater variety than on M1.

They visited and worshiped at three temples every day, at least. And dined at a different place every evening, following it with nightly excursions which helped them attain a better sense of the material, intellectual, and spiritual culture of M2.

Will and Saro spent one whole day together, roaming Will's usual haunts. Saro finally heard the story of Will's last days on Urantia, his ordeal and death as a prisoner of war, and his subsequent adventures on M1 and M2. Will had volunteered, and was now serving, as counselor to others who had died in wars or under other grievous circumstances, been resurrected, passed through M1, but were still having trouble adjusting.

On that same day, while Saro and Will traveled about, Joy and Kala visited sites of Joy's artistic team projects. Joy also told Kala about the wonderful shock she had awakening in a young, healthy, cancer-free body in Resurrection Hall. "I still give thanks everyday for eternal good health," declared Joy.

Joy and Kala talked about Joy's first assignments on M1 embellishing its artistry, and her present work on M2 with the title, Assistant to Celestial Artisans. She was working on a team of hundreds who create gigantic morontia sculpture. Immediately on beholding morontia art forms Joy felt an affinity for celestial creativity. And she was now contemplating joining the Artisan Corps, making a one thousand year commitment. They discussed the pluses and minuses of such a commitment. Joy was soon to make her choice. Her only reservation was about the length of it. Kala didn't want to advise or influence her one way or the other.

Finally Joy said, "I know a thousand years here is like a day on Paradise. And there's no shortage of days in eternity."

After much traveling around M2, and by previous arrangement, Kala and Joy, Saro, Will, and their two cousins, met at Kala's parents' residence on the evening of their sixth day. The eight of them sat for a "homemade" meal. The art of food preparation is well refined on M2, and Kala's parents are regarded as consummate professionals in that art. Saro raved over the taste, as did the other guests. Afterward they settled comfortably for conversation.

They talked much about the service in which Kala's parents were involved, engaging and assisting ascenders who were experiencing intellectual conflicts and mental disharmony that resulted from difficulty in grasping the significance and use of morontia mota. Mota is introduced on M1, and studied on M2. Her parents had an exceptional grasp of it, and a talent for teaching it. And they thoroughly enjoyed their work.

Will's and Saro's cousins described their work on M2 as, "government agents." One of them explained, "We are volunteers on a commission that selects potential leaders coming up from Urantia. Ones who have shown an ability to lead, like you two. Too bad you aren't staying on M2. We would draft you." They laughed and then had a long discussion about the way the mansion worlds are managed. They also reminisced and pieced together more of their common experiences at the many family reunions that punctuated their unique lives on Urantia.

They ended the dinner party with a touching Last Supper re-enactment and a short period of prayer and worship. It was well past midnight when the group broke up and returned to their abodes.

On the morning of the seventh day Kala, Saro, their relatives, and Solonia met at daybreak outside a large amphitheater not far from Kala's parents' residence. Kala and Saro were joyously anticipating this day long presentation of Jesus' life and teachings by the Celestial Artisans. It had been their habit for five decades to read Part IV of *The Urantia Book* every year between Christmas and Easter. And every year they discussed the possibility and potential of taking the beautiful story out of the text and putting it onto Urantia's movie screens, where new visions of the Master could be presented to the whole planet, and not just to a small minority of literate adults.

Solonia remained with the group the whole day, enjoying it every bit as much as they did. By daybreak of the next morning (there were twenty-one intermissions) every theater goer was filled to capacity with love for this God who condescended to live a life in the flesh in order that he might come close to humanity and speak the truth of the reality of the God of All, to actually become one of the lowest of his ascending creatures.

Saro and Kala were so taken up by the performance that they had to give vent to tears more than once during the presentation. It was everything they dreamed such an audacious presentation should be. Indeed, much more. And now they had a clearer idea of what went on behind the scenes, on the celestial level, as the Master's life unfolded on Urantia.

When the presentation ended, almost the entire group betook themselves to worship in a temple adjacent to the amphitheater. Many were so moved as to weep for joy and pain after beholding the spectacle of the Master's life in such fine detail, and as they absorbed the meaning and value of the incarnation of such a loving God as Our Father in the person of Michael, Nebadon's sovereign.

After the worship session Kala and Saro's group took a transport to a spacious and strikingly beautiful garden home, a mansion unto itself. A friend of Solonia's was absent and offered it as a post-presentation retreat. None needed rest; indeed they were all energized in spirit, mind, and body. Evidently Jesus' life presentations have a powerful effect on everyone and it is common practice to retreat after experiencing a presentation.

Saro and Kala thoroughly enjoyed spending the rest of the day in the company of their relatives, in the afterglow of viewing the greatest of all stories. During this time the group discussed many of the details, events, and teachings of the Master's life.

They revealed to themselves and the others their deepest spiritual feelings after seeing his life depicted in such vivid terms. They spent considerable time talking over certain aspects of his complex teachings, especially his parables.

They also talked about personal and cosmic destiny, from their position on Mansonia all the way up to the great mother of time and space, the Supreme Being. And then, when daylight began to fade, contemplation turned to play. They made merry and rejoiced with music and dance until the next morning.

Just after daybreak the trio said farewell to Will, Joy, Kala's parents and Saro's cousins. They wished each other the greatest success and Godspeed in their respective endeavors, until they should meet again somewhere, sometime, on one of the mansion worlds, their homes for the immediate future.

On day nine the pair took no excursions and made no schedule. It was a day of rest and relaxation. The only activity was exploring their temporary lodging's neighborhood, on foot and by boat, in between frequent periods of worship.

Day ten, their last day of liberty on M2, Saro and Kala spent coming to know its indigenous beings, some of whom they chanced to meet traveling between worship sessions at the three temples they had chosen to visit. And where they could make friends or minister to fellow ascenders, they did so, 'as they passed by.'

Solonia continued to be an invaluable aid and translator in their interactions with mansion world natives, fellow ascenders, and spirit beings of diverse orders. They very much enjoyed M2, and looked forward to visiting it again soon, but then they will be touring as fused morontians and class leaders.

By pre-arrangement Kala's grandparents met them on M3's sea of glass. After the four had embraced and introduced Solonia, Kala's grandmother invited the trio to stay at their residence, near the headquarters of the Mansion World Teachers. First the group proceeded to the sphere's temple of seventy wings where Kala and Saro submitted themselves to their second adjustment in the System Co-ordinators' transition chambers.

Just as predicted, the previous adjustment did have its effects in seven days. Kala likened it to a "miniature resurrection." In fact the pair was adjusting magnificently to their rapid transition. And while they were cruising smoothly through outer reality, even assisting others as they went, they were also taking greater and greater strides in their inner lives. They and their Adjusters were working within to remove the remaining hurdles and end their period of betrothal, to begin life eternal in surety and reality, to unite as one forever.

In the transport pod on the way to Kala's grandparents' residence Solonia recited her well-memorized speech to ascending pilgrims touring M3 for the first time:

"Mansonia the third is the headquarters of the Mansion World Teachers. Though they function on all seven of the mansion spheres, they maintain their group headquarters at the center of the school circles of world number three. There are millions of these instructors on the mansion and higher morontia worlds. (47:5.1)

"On this sphere more positive educational work is begun.

The training of the first two mansion worlds is mostly of a deficiency nature — negative — in that it has to do with supplementing the experience of the life in the flesh. On this third mansion world the survivors really begin their progressive morontia culture. The chief purpose of this training is to enhance the understanding of the correlation of morontia mota and mortal logic, the co-ordination of morontia mota and human philosophy. Surviving mortals now gain practical insight into true metaphysics. This is the real introduction to the intelligent comprehension of cosmic meanings and universe interrelationships. The culture of the third mansion world partakes of the nature of the post-bestowal Son age of a normal inhabited planet." (47:5.3)

'We'll have to visit the Mansion World Teachers," Kala said. Saro nodded whole-hearted agreement.

When the trio had settled in, Solonia departed to officially register at the sphere's headquarters and meet with friends stationed on M3. Kala and Saro agreed to inform Solonia when their liberty was fully planned. The rest of the pair's first day on M3 was spent at her grandparents' abode preparing a meal and discussing a host of topics.

That morning the four of them gathered a large variety of vegetables, seeds, and nuts from a garden that was created by the locals and tended by resident spornagia. Bringing their harvest in, they sat around a sculptured table made of a lustrous crystal material shaped in the form of M3's sea of glass. They talked as Kala's grandparents instructed them in the preparation of morontia produce. Her grandfather informed them that a casual gathering had been planned that evening in order to introduce the pair to some of their M3 friends and workmates.

"Gram and Pop, I'm still having trouble seeing you in bodies as young as ours," Kala confessed. "I can't look at you as grandparents anymore."

"Good," said Gram. "We are simply sisters forever now."

"Guess that makes us brothers," Saro said to Pop. They smiled broadly and shook hands.

Kala said, "I feel like giving you new names."

Gram replied, "Why don't you use Gram and Pop until we receive our permanent names. It brings fond recollections of good times on Urantia."

Saro wanted to know more about their service in the System's probationary nurseries. The pair missed seeing and interacting with children.

Pop said, "We maintain residence on M3, but we commute to the nursery on the Finaliters' world. We serve with a special division of ministers. Kala, you recall that we, during our latter years, worked in hospices on Urantia, right? It's similar but here we attempt to help the older children — not the aged, sick and dying — of the probationary nurseries in making their final decision about eternal life."

"I can recall reading about this. And wondering why anyone would consider rejecting life." Kala thought for a moment and added, "Your work must be very rewarding, but isn't it heart-breaking when a child chooses ending life?"

"It is both rewarding and difficult," replied Gram. "When a young one decides to live and accept the divine path, we all rejoice. But when one chooses not to, it's disappointing and heart wrenching for our whole group. Of course the parent, or parents, suffer the most."

"So, you both must really enjoy the challenge of this kind of service," Saro said.

"We do," replied Gram. "And it's the one and only chance they have. On Urantia we believed there's always another chance after resurrection. But here, if we fail to convince these young ones of the purpose, meaning, and value of the gift of eternal life, a gift from God on Paradise, a loving God who is calling on them to be daughters and sons, that choice ends life permanently. Not by divine decree, but by the person's own choosing.

"But if we're successful, the young one transports to M1 and begins the ascension regime. We're committed to this service for at least ten years, and it's been quite an education; somewhat similar to working with the dying on Urantia. Except of course, we know death here is irrevocable for anyone who finally and fully rejects the gift of life eternal."

Kala asked, "What do the wards offer as a reason for declining eternity?"

"Amazingly, some show little or no interest. They have no appetite for the myriad challenges and spiritual hurdles that face ascenders, and no affinity for the goal of achieving perfection over billions of years, and across a billion-plus worlds. Some can't understand why they weren't born perfect, as are Havona and Paradise citizens. Others can't see the point of all this cosmic activity if it doesn't really mean anything when everything is said and done. And some others object to the confinement of eternal service under a God they can't see and sometimes, tragically, don't want to know or love. And a sad few display outright contempt for both God and the Paradise journey."

Kala and Saro were thinking of their grown children still on Urantia, and took comfort in the recollection of the Evangel's statement that their children had already made the decision to accept the gift of life eternal in God's good service.

After dining on the luscious items the four had prepared earlier, Kala and Saro socialized with the diverse and fascinating array of guests invited by Gram and Pop. This helped them realize yet more fully that each world presents a broad variety of upward shifts, both within and without, and on the physical, intellectual, and spiritual levels.

When the guests had departed the pair strolled the starlit neighborhood and thought over their itinerary for the remaining nine days on M3. After a bit they sat on the ground under a massive tree with delicious fruit hanging and laying everywhere. The fruit's richness appealed to the taste of friendly, adorable, morontian animals, and ascending pilgrims alike. It made a perfect dessert after their family meal at Gram and Pop's. Saro remarked about how sensitivity to the taste of everything was improving with each step up the mansion world ladder. In fact they both noted all senses were improving quickly, that their sensory arrays had added new dimensions and revealed more and finer subtleties following both adjustments.

After researching the countless activities and venues on M3, the pair confirmed their plan to visit the headquarters of the Mansion World Teachers, and while there, audit a cherubim sponsored Melchizedek symposium on morontia mota. They planned to worship at all the major temples. And of course they allotted time for flying over M3 on the backs of the great passenger birds.

~ Chapter 16 ~
Touring M3, First Visit To Jerusem

The theme of the Melchizedek symposium was mota. The pair did very much enjoy hearing the Melchizedek speak. His words seemed always to be on the leading edge of their understanding and grasp of mota. He said, in part:

"Reason is the understanding technique of the sciences; faith is the insight technique of religion; mota is the technique of the morontia level. Mota is a super-material reality sensitivity which is beginning to compensate incomplete growth, having for its substance knowledge-reason and for its essence faith-insight. Mota is a super-philosophical reconciliation of divergent reality perception which is non-attainable by material personalities; it is predicated, in part, on the experience of having survived the material life of the flesh. (103:6.7)

"In the mortal state, nothing can be absolutely proved; both science and religion are predicated on assumptions. On the morontia level, the postulates of both science and religion are capable of partial proof by mota logic. On the spiritual level of maximum status, the need for finite proof gradually vanishes before the actual experience of and with reality; but even then there is much beyond the finite that remains unproved. (103:7.10)

"Providence becomes increasingly discernible as men reach upward from the material to the spiritual. The attainment of completed spiritual insight enables the ascending personality to detect harmony in what was theretofore chaos. Even morontia mota represents a real advance in this direction." (118:10.19)

After the day at the symposium, the pair met Solonia and

dined with several of the other mota symposium attendees. The group engaged in discussions about a basic definition of mota. A consensus evolved that mota is simply a sensitivity to truth.

That evening, they took a long flight over M3 on the backs of the adorable passenger birds.

Saro and Kala decided to spend the rest their M3 liberty in the company of Gram and Pop, staying with them and going along on their daily ministry to children of indecision in the probationary nursery of T1, Transition World Number One, the Finaliters' world. They all four did so love children. And in this situation Kala and Saro also felt deep sorrow and a compelling urge to do something when faced with the reality of the choice of rejection of eternal life by some of the young ones. But, as observers, they did not presume to intrude or offer advice.

They also decided to put off their visit to the System's capital, Jerusem, until arriving on M4, agreeing that time spent observing Gram's and Pop's ministry on T1 has great value. The pair truly enjoyed their days on this remarkable transition world, one that differs markedly from the mansion worlds, and in ways they could never have imagined. At their evening dinners back on M3 with Gram and Pop, the four discussed the day's counseling sessions with the probationary wards, and other difficulties of the ascension career that face young ones if and when they choose life.

When it was time to enseraphim for M4, Gram and Pop flew with the trio to M3's sea of glass. As Saro and Kala took their last look — for a while at least — they thought about how much more sophisticated, complex, and spiritually oriented each mansion world is. M1 and M2 now seemed somewhat quaint compared to M3 and the Finaliters' World.

As they approached the spaceport Kala asked her grandparents, "Do you know what you'll do after your ten year commitment?"

"Why, follow in your footsteps, of course!" exclaimed Pop. They laughed. "You two are an inspiration for us all."

"Thank you," muttered Saro and Kala.

Gram added, "We will make it to M7 and someday fuse, but there's no rush, no hurry, no fear of failure. The Evangels recommended we remain on each mansion world as long as there is need of our services. And that's what we've done. I thank God for the opportunity."

"Do you two plan to separate, ever?" Kala asked.

"Do you?" Pop answered.

Kala replied, "The Evangels didn't indicate we should part, at least as long as we're in Mansonia. But there really is no point in guessing what might or might not happen after we've fused and before we leave Mansonia, is there? That could be thousands of years."

Pop answered, "We came to the same conclusion. We like being together, so speculation about separating is fruitless and unnecessary. But we are taught the fewer personal plans we make concerning others, the less chance there will be for disappointment. And you know as well as anyone, no matter what happens, no matter how far separated, eternal friendships endure; cosmic relationships remain and grow. Look at Andon and Fonta. They've been working together as long as the human race has existed."

It was a joyful departure. Saro and Kala thanked their hosts for everything from delectable sustenance to comfortable lodging to the enlightening experience observing their unusual work in the System's probationary nurseries.

After landing on M4 the three of them went to the System Co-ordinators for Saro's and Kala's third adjustment. They then summoned transportation to their assigned quarters in the Melchizedek sector. As they flew, the pair watched the scenery below and Solonia reeled off the Companions' standard description of M4 for pilgrims on excursion.

"When you arrive on the fourth mansion world, you have well entered upon the morontia career; you have progressed a long way from the initial material existence. Now are you given

permission to make visits to transition world number four, there to become familiar with the headquarters and training schools of the superangels, including the Brilliant Evening Stars. (47:6.1)

"Through the good offices of these superangels of the fourth transition world the morontia visitors are enabled to draw very close to the various orders of the Sons of God during the periodic visits to Jerusem, for new sectors of the system capital are gradually opening up to the advancing mortals as they make these repeated visits to the headquarters world. New grandeurs are progressively unfolding to the expanding minds of these ascenders. (47:6.1)

"On the fourth mansonia the individual ascender more fittingly finds his place in the group working and class functions of the morontia life. Ascenders here develop increased appreciation of the broadcasts and other phases of local universe culture and progress. (47:6.2)

"It is during the period of training on world number four that the ascending mortals are really first introduced to the demands and delights of the true social life of morontia creatures. And it is indeed a new experience for evolutionary creatures to participate in social activities which are predicated neither on personal aggrandizement nor on self-seeking conquest. A new social order is being introduced, one based on the understanding sympathy of mutual appreciation, the unselfish love of mutual service, and the overmastering motivation of the realization of a common and supreme destiny — the Paradise goal of worshipful and divine perfection. Ascenders are all becoming self-conscious of God-knowing, God-revealing, God-seeking, and God-finding." (47:6.3)

After Solonia had escorted them to their new quarters, she once again took leave to register their arrival and contact friends stationed on M4. Before she left they arranged to meet the next morning to travel to Jerusem.

After Kala and Saro had surveyed their lodging, they roamed the immediate area to get a sense of M4's indigenous life and morontia culture. The mansion worlds are not alike but certain consistencies are obvious. The living and working arrangements are always designed within circles, triangles, rectangles, and squares. And all worlds are heated and lighted the same way, they each have a host of glorious temples in which pilgrims may progress in worship, gratitude, and thanksgiving. All have beautiful waterways, lakes, rivers, and canals. And all mansion worlds have gardens, parks, and recreational amenities; gradually increasing in charm and allure as pilgrims ascend from M1 to M7.

The pair strolled silently for a long while, observing and noting the many beings of diverse kind and form, most of whom they were seeing for the first time. Kala and Saro discovered yet again, and to their unending amazement, that life is considerably richer in spiritual orientation, social culture, and physical materials with each advance up the mansion regime.

Saro broke their silence, asking Kala, "My love, should we make another use of our pilot permits?"

They spent the remainder of the day soaring over, landing, and exploring many of the nearby attractions of M4 while Solonia reconnected with her M4 friends. Saro and Kala were pleased their journey afforded Solonia personal time on each of the mansion worlds. Her assistance and presence was invaluable. They were continually realizing and appreciating the depth of experience and range of skills displayed by their congenial companion. Solonia had, in the short time of their acquaintance, already earned their trust, friendship, and admiration.

Early the next morning, well before daybreak, the pair was up and out. They worshiped at a nearby temple first. Increasingly the two were feeling rapid expansions of inner life smoothly and simultaneously merging with their quickly progressing outer life. The inner and outer were becoming a harmonious flow on multiple levels; dynamic yet stable. And they were finding and exploring new arenas of thinking, feeling, and acting with each day's passing.

Just as the pair was exiting the temple, Solonia greeted them.

"How'd you know we were here?" Saro asked with a smile.

"I have friends," she answered slyly. "Are you two ready to enseraphim for Jerusem?"

"We are!" they declared emphatically.

Right after the trio arrived on Jerusem, Kala and Saro decided to take another bird flight. Their first impression was of its vastness and level of development compared to the mansions and T1. Immediately they felt that Jerusem must be the most beautiful and well developed of all the System's spheres. The intensity of activity and concentration of structures, promenades, sculpture and art, struck them deeply. Jerusem is one hundred times larger than M1, Saro recalled. But they noted no difference in gravity's pull.

Solonia was waiting when they returned to the aviary. "What do you think of the System's capital?"

Saro answered, "It's all right — if one likes divine magnificence, cosmic grandeur, unimaginable variety, lavish gardens, and transcendent beauty. A bit ostentatious for my refined sensibilities." Solonia and Kala laughed at Saro's pretended haughtiness.

Solonia informed the pair, "We happened to arrive on the day the System's chief administrator, Lanaforge, is holding a conclave here on Jerusem's administrative mount. The day-long meetings are informal and unforgettable. I think you will not regret attending in the least. The meeting will give you a glimpse of System administrative procedures, their design, problems, and solutions."

They took Solonia's suggestion, and were not disappointed. Almost immediately Saro and Kala could sense the sublime fraternity between the System Sovereign and the mass of beings in attendance, most of whom he governed. How much different, they thought, than the general relations that exist between the governors and the governed on Urantia.

The pair marveled at the fact that they were in the presence of one who replaced the rebel Lanonandek son who led the third rebellion against God and Michael in Nebadon. They couldn't help thinking that Lanaforge is truly a mighty son of God, a genuine, magnanimous, sincere, child of Michael and the Divine Mother, a gracious person, and quite obviously a brilliant being and benevolent ruler.

"I recall studying him," Kala said. "It was Lanaforge who was faithful in an earlier rebellion. During Nebadon's second uprising he took charge and persuaded many from following the sophistry of the rebel chiefs. His wisdom, loyalty and efforts saved a swathe of beings, from inhabitants of the lowest planets, to angels on the System's headquarters. And he did it all in spite of being out-ranked by the lead rebel."

In answer to a question from a visiting star student about the final tally of the rebellion on the System headquarters, Lanaforge said:

"Not a single Jerusem citizen was lost. Every ascendant mortal survived the fiery trial and emerged from the crucial test triumphant and altogether victorious." (53:7.12)

All that day they listened and learned as Lanaforge and his six sibling administrators spoke informally with a great variety of Jerusem citizens and others at the gathering. Saro and Kala were fascinated and informed by what they learned of System culture and function, from both citizens and their leaders.

That evening, after the conclave, the trio enjoyed a sumptuous meal with many of those who attended it. They dined at a gloriously beautiful and inviting service center adjacent to Jerusem's offices of the Executive Council. The pair used the opportunity to converse intimately with a few of the average citizens and lower level administrators. Kala and Saro quickly realized that Jerusem is a physical and spiritual wonderland, a divinely inspired and created culture of vast diversity, exquisite beauty, and spiritual elevation.

That night, Solonia took the pair on a flying tour of the

System's extensive headquarters. As they circled over a brightly lit residential area she recited the names of the current heads of Jerusem's government who reside there, the seven Lanonandek Sons: *"Lanaforge, Mansurotia, Sadib, Holdant, Vilton, Fortant, and Hanavard."* (45:3.1)

"Who does come up with their names?" Saro quipped.

Solonia pointed to a great ring of seven concentric circles.

"There you see the angels' residential area. At the center is where John the Revelator saw the *'four and twenty elders sitting, clothed in white raiment.'* (45:4.1)

"You no doubt recall that the twenty-four members of the Urantia advisory council are Michael's agents working on Urantia related projects. But do you recall the sixteen individuals who were listed?"

"Not all," Saro confessed.

"Name them please," said Kala.

"Onagar, Mansant, Onamonalonton, Orlandof, Porshunta, Singlangton, Fantad, Orvonon, Adam, Eve, Enoch, Moses, Elijah, Machiventa Melchizedek, John the Baptist, and a Midwayer named, 1-2-3 the First." (45:4.2)

"Fascinating to think of that much concentrated human and morontian experience, working together in one place. And for the good of Urantia," Kala said thoughtfully.

Solonia went on, *"The great divisions of celestial life have their headquarters and immense preserves on Jerusem, including the various orders of divine Sons, high spirits, superangels, angels, and midway creatures. The central abode of this wonderful sector is the chief temple of the Material Sons."* (45:5.1)

She added, "One of the biggest attractions on this sphere is the Adam and Eve family estates, wherein new pairs of material sons are created, trained, and chosen for service on the evolutionary worlds."

The trio decided to stay overnight on Jerusem; arranging

lodging with Solonia's friends. The next day, with Solonia's connections, they fulfilled another deferred dream. They were invited to visit the home of a Material Son and Daughter. The Adamic area on Jerusem has one thousand centers of family estates.

On the way there they talked about the physicality, spirituality, and culture of these marvelously handsome, divinely descended, and glowing creatures who do so enjoy creating families, growing gardens, teaching music, producing art, reciting poetry, making good humor, and in general, broadening culture for the greater good of all families.

The Material Sons and Daughters were plainly visible to Kala's and Saro's morontia eyes. The pair had seen them first on T1, at the probationary nurseries, but had not yet interacted with them. Kala was recalling this statement,

"The probationary nursery itself is supervised by one thousand couples of Material Sons and Daughters, volunteers from the Jerusem colony." (45:6.9)

Saro and Kala well noted what magnificent creatures these 'material' beings are; violet in complexion, quite tall and robust in body, interesting persons all, yet diverse in personality. And every one of them is focused primarily on home and family life, child-rearing and garden-building. And what splendid children they raise and what marvelous gardens they build. Seeing the way the Adamites live made Kala and Saro think what Urantia's first garden of Eden might have been like, before it collapsed in default. And what Urantia could — someday will — be like; another lovely and unique patch in God's cosmic garden.

Solonia reminded them, "The Adams and Eves are children of Michael alone. You well know the teachings that they are sexually endowed and the parents of a race of specially designed beings. There are more than 161 million Adamites in Nebadon. They are permanent inhabitants of the System, and their eventual aim is self-governance. Right now they are overseen by the higher orders of sonship, the Lanonandeks, the Vorondadeks, and Melchizedeks."

Saro searched for a quote he recalled, about the Adamic families and ascenders' leisure time on Jerusem: *"Mortal survivors spend much of their leisure on the system capital observing and studying the life habits and conduct of these superior semiphysical sex creatures, for these citizens of Jerusem are the immediate sponsors and mentors of the mortal survivors from the time they attain citizenship on the headquarters world until they take leave for Edentia."* (45:6.2)

~ Chapter 17 ~
Adamic Estate and Broadcast Center

"This is the quote I recall most vividly, about one of the rehabilitation services Adams and Eves provide for certain ascending mortals." Kala read it.

"Sex experience in a physical sense is past for these ascenders, but in close association with the Material Sons and Daughters, both individually and as members of their families, these sex-deficient mortals are enabled to compensate the social, intellectual, emotional, and spiritual aspects of their deficiency. Thus are all those humans whom circumstances or bad judgment deprived of the benefits of advantageous sex association on the evolutionary worlds, here on the system capitals afforded full opportunity to acquire these essential mortal experiences in close and loving association with the supernal Adamic sex creatures of permanent residence on the system capitals." (45:6.3)

Solonia gave them information about another service provided for ascenders by Adam and Eve families, regarding the teaching of principles and methods of self-governance. She said in part:

"The Melchizedek Sons conduct upward of thirty different educational centers on Jerusem. These training schools begin with the college of self-evaluation and end with the schools of Jerusem citizenship, wherein the Material Sons and Daughters join with the Melchizedeks and others in their supreme effort to qualify the mortal survivors for the assumption of the high responsibilities of representative government. The entire universe is organized and administered on the representative plan. Representative government is the divine ideal of self-

government among non-perfect beings." (45:7.3)

"The vote cast at a Jerusem election by any one personality has a value ranging from one up to one thousand. Jerusem citizens are thus classified in accordance with their mota achievement." (45:7.6)

They landed at an estate where Solonia is well known, a typical Adamic family home where Saro and Kala may watch and learn from these beautiful beings who are the last in a line of divinity that stretches from the heights of Paradise down to tiny quarantined worlds like Urantia.

As the trio walked toward the estate's central edifice, they talked about the array of training ascenders can receive while living with Adams, Eves, and their progeny. Solonia told them, as she had said to many others who toured the Adamic estates, "Ex-humans can compensate for their deficiencies in social, intellectual, emotional aspects of life as they live and serve in loving association with Adams and Eves."

The mother Eve and father Adam of the estate were away at a reunion of their order on Edentia, the constellation capital. The first-born son and daughter were in charge at that moment. The trio was given free rein to explore and visit with family members and staff. While touring the estate Kala and Saro encountered dozens of the Adamic children and young adults working the gardens, with help from the spornagia. One of the more mature couples they spoke with was making ready to attend a System Melchizedek school, preparatory to bestowing themselves on a race of beings who are coming of age on an evolutionary world.

"Do you know which planet?" Kala asked.

"World 615 is nearly ready to receive an Adam and Eve. But there are several couples competing," answered the female of the two.

Saro wanted to know, "What type of being will you be up-stepping?"

"A one-brained race, on a world not too different from

Urantia. It is under quarantine still. We expect it to be a challenge. That is one of the reasons we volunteered."

All the Adamite children they met wanted to hear stories from Kala's and Saro's lives on a quarantined evolutionary world. And they wanted to know all about Adamic life. The pair spent most of the day exchanging stories and information with these curious, intelligent, 'material' beings. Each of them enjoyed these personal exchanges, especially Kala and Saro. The experience was another unforgettable one they wished very much to expand upon during their repeat ascension.

They were offered an invitation to stay the night at the Adamic estate, which they gladly and graciously accepted. That evening after dining on a great variety of excellently prepared goods from the estate's immense and bountiful gardens, many family members gathered, as they do every evening, to make music, sing, dance, and put on instructive skits for the little ones.

Kala and Saro delighted in the company of this amazing family whose members so well exemplify the heights to which family culture might rise. And they used the opportunity to learn about and try many of the morontia musical instruments the family kept. Before the night was over the pair was entertaining them all with impromptu compositions recalled from their careers as classical musicians on Urantia.

The next morning the pair said farewell to their hosts, almost tearfully. Such was the bond they had made with this family in a short time. They embraced the gathered family members, said adoring so-longs, and promised to visit again.

After the trio boarded a pod Solonia said, "You have made more eternal friends."

"What a lovely time, what a delightful family!" Kala declared. "Visiting an ideal family situation like that gives new meaning to ideal. I can't help thinking about how far along Urantia would be if the first garden hadn't failed. Adam and Eve might still be there, fostering greater and greater families like that one, preparing for the next descending Son to take Urantia to the dawn of Light and Life...but then if the garden hadn't failed, Michael might not have chosen Urantia for his seventh bestowal."

After a moment's reflection on Kala's statement, Saro asked Solonia, "How was the news of the fall of Urantia's first Eden received on Mansonia?"

"We were all watching of course. From the beginning Urantia's Adam and Eve faced an uphill struggle, that was indisputable. They were cosmically alone on a quarantined world. They were born and trained biologists, not administrators. They met defeat at every turn for over a hundred years, until madness touched them. Still, disappointment was the initial reaction to their error. But then, before long, it became a cornerstone of teaching on how to choose wisely in such a trying situation. Now it is regarded as a fortuitous occurrence and an education for all, not just the Adams and Eves."

Saro asked, "Adam and Eve are still here on Jerusem, serving on the council of twenty-four elders?"

"They are," Solonia answered. "I count them among my friends."

"Maybe you will introduce us one day," Kala said.

"I will, and gladly so."

"Where shall we go now?" Kala wondered.

Saro replied with a smile, "Shall we repair to the Jerusem broadcast center, my love?"

"Is it broken?"

Solonia glanced at them quizzically, "Urantian humor?"

Kala and Saro watched as the charming Adamic estate disappeared behind them. Shortly thereafter the transport pod sat down at a massive gate leading to the broadcast center. The pair peered inside and stood in amazement until Solonia broke their gaze and prompted them to enter.

After a moment to regain their composure, they slowly walked into the System's massive communication hub. Billions of beings rely on the broadcast center for everything from local happenings to news from Orvonton and the other six superuniverses, even to events occurring on Havona and Paradise. Kala and Saro decided to sit for a moment just to observe the broadcast center in full service. The pair compared revelations about Jerusem's vast and busiest facility to the reality of it. Saro read:

"This Jerusem broadcast-receiving station is encircled by an enormous amphitheater, constructed of scintillating materials largely unknown on Urantia and seating over five billion beings — material and morontia — besides accommodating innumerable spirit personalities. It is the favorite diversion for all Jerusem to spend their leisure at the broadcast station, there to learn of the welfare and state of the universe. And this is the only planetary activity which is not slowed down during the recession of light." (46:3.2)

"It's fascinating to think of billions of God-knowing, God-loving beings in one place at the same time," mused Kala. "And here we are!"

The broadcast center did not disappoint the pair. In fact, it was all but overwhelming. They spent the rest of the day amid those billions of beings of vastly diverse orders who were also viewing and reporting the endless news and activities being received by and transmitted from the System's communications center. Never before had they felt the joy or known the satisfactions of following the myriad events, activities, and surprises unfolding inside other superuniverses and on Paradise.

As they moved toward the center of the amphitheater, Kala and Saro were forming the same cosmic impression: The Universe is indeed a marvelous, stupendous creation of limitless diversity and divinely appointed progress — notwithstanding the fact that the four outer space levels are as yet uninhabited and the Grand Universe is not close to being settled in light and life. They were realizing how young the Master Universe is.

This realization reminded Kala of Jesus' parable about hirelings who began work at different times of the day, yet received the same pay. It sparked an image in Saro's mind, of a far-away vision of the completed Master Universe in seven rings, each sparkling with light and life in all its aspects and dimensions.

Saro then thought of future local developments, "Imagine what Jerusem might be when all seven rings around Paradise are fully inhabited, settled, and perfected. It could perform a totally different function. Have you thought, or been instructed about events that far ahead, Solonia?"

She answered with a humble smile, "Since the settling of the entire Master Universe in light and life is so very far off, all of my speculations about it have broken down in a sea of variables, a flood of permutations, and any number of unforeseen inundations of divine providence."

Solonia stayed with the pair all day and into the evening. She too enjoyed perusing the latest news from Edentia and other spheres of the local universe, especially news from Salvington with details on the recent doings of the Divine Minister. Finally the pair decided to take a break. They had absorbed much valuable and fascinating information about the vast and mysterious universe in which we all live and grow.

As they were leaving, Kala asked, "Solonia, where were you during Michael's morontia ascension?"

"Great throngs met and followed him everywhere he visited and spoke. I was privileged to be among them, it was a transcendently joyous and inspiring time. In fact, Jerusem's memorial is nearby, in the Circles of the Sons."

"Let's go, Saro," Kala said.

They had encountered the first Michael Memorial on M1. Immediately on arriving at the Jerusem memorial the pair felt the same wondrous presence and comfort of the Master's Spirit they had felt at the welcoming ceremony. Saro located the lines he was now recalling about this one:

"These circular reservations of the Sons occupy an enormous area, and until nineteen hundred years ago there existed a great open space at its center. This central region is now occupied by the Michael memorial, completed some five hundred years ago. Four hundred and ninety-five years ago, when this temple was dedicated, Michael was present in person, and all Jerusem heard the touching story of the Master Son's bestowal on Urantia, the least of Satania. The Michael memorial is now the center of all activities embraced in the modified management of the system occasioned by Michael's bestowal, including most of the more recently transplanted Salvington activities. The memorial staff consists of over one million personalities." (46:5.19)

That night the trio returned to M4. There they dined and then worshiped at a nearby temple. Afterward Solonia said good night and the pair retired for sound and solid rest after two days of near continuous and highly stimulating activity.

The remainder of their fourth mansion world liberty was spent exploring it and Transition World Four. On M4 they saw evidence of the flowering of true social brotherhood and spiritual equality. They found a much greater awareness of the existence and essential role of the Supreme Being. Solonia went along on each of their excursions, offering information and insight about the citizens of M4, most of whom are particularly schooled in practicing justice and living mercy.

On T4, the Superangels' World, they met and engaged the Brilliant Evening Stars, sibling angels of the two who welcomed Saro, Kala, and 200,000 other resurrectees at the Banquet Hall reception. While on T4 they worshiped with angels of diverse orders and sampled the rich flavor of high angelic culture, as much as they could visualize of it.

Each of the seven sub-satellites of T4 provided the pair with additional insights into the angelic realm, a fascinating spectrum of beings whose main mission and first pursuit is service, and the more challenging the service, the better. The charm, power, and abilities of all the angels they had so far encountered astounded and intrigued them to the point of pledging to return with a great class of ascenders from Urantia, for a comprehensive education on angelic service and culture.

With each advance, Kala and Saro were finding themselves more and more interested in knowing and speaking the common languages of the local universe. And they noticed that the ability to learn was accelerating with each body/mind adjustment. Solonia proved to be a first rate language tutor which meant they could receive her excellent instruction during their time confined to travel pods. It helped that they very much enjoyed each others' company.

Kala asked, "In how many languages are you fluent, Solonia?"

"All of the System's and much of Nebadon's. Several hundred thousand perhaps. I learned many during a ten thousand year stint in the corps of Interpreters and Translators. They are, as you probably recall, another of the seven general service activities of Morontia Companions. My mind seems well suited for learning and retaining them."

During their travels around M4 the pair also discovered it to be a world where ascenders find their roles in the slow moving class formations, and where they begin to evince an increasing interest in morontia life and its progressive nature. On M4 ascenders experience both the requirements and joys of morontia culture. This is a world where ascenders become self-conscious of having found and knowing God.

~ Chapter 18 ~
Touring M5, T5, M6, T6 and M7

As soon as the trio arrived on M5, Kala and Saro received their fourth adjustment, then ensconced themselves in the Melchizedek sector while Solonia reported their itinerary to headquarters. The pair was very curious about this mansion world because it corresponds to the early stages of light and life on the evolutionary worlds. And right away they sensed it had a cultural flavor similar to Jerusem's.

After strolling their area, and when Solonia returned, the trio began making a tentative plan for their M5 stay. In the discussions about it, Solonia said, "From here you can visit the Son's headquarters world, T5. The Melchizedek, Vorondadek, Lanonandek, and creature trinitized sons reside there. It is an especially fascinating place for us universe daughters."

Solonia recited the tour guide's introductory speech about M5 for ascending arrivals:

"On the fifth mansonia you begin to learn of the constellation study worlds. Here you meet the first of the instructors who begin to prepare you for the subsequent constellation sojourn. More of this preparation continues on worlds six and seven, while the finishing touches are supplied in the sector of the ascending mortals on Jerusem. (47:7.4)

"A real birth of cosmic consciousness takes place on mansonia number five. You are becoming universe minded. This is indeed a time of expanding horizons. It is beginning to dawn upon the enlarging minds of the ascending mortals that some stupendous and magnificent, some supernal and divine, destiny awaits all who complete the progressive Paradise ascension, which has been so laboriously but so joyfully and

auspiciously begun. At about this point the average mortal ascender begins to manifest bona fide experiential enthusiasm for the Havona ascent. Study is becoming voluntary, unselfish service natural, and worship spontaneous. A real morontia character is budding; a real morontia creature is evolving." (47:7.5)

Solonia added, "And this is the world where ascending classes are schooled in the superuniverse's language. Jerusem citizens are proficient in the tongues of both Nebadon and Uversa."

After considering their many options, the pair settled on spending the first half of their ten-day liberty on M5 and the second half on T5. While on M5 they took an extensive bird flight, visiting many of its temples of sublime and stunning beauty. They truly enjoyed its magnificent morontia architecture, its functional and ornamental artistry on an even grander scale than the lower mansions.

They worshiped with visible and invisible beings of diverse orders while on M5, each time soaring a bit higher on their souls' out-stretched wings. Solonia was good to keep the pair apprised of the presence of certain beings they could not yet visualize.

On M5 they continued to make the cultural rounds each evening, attending concerts, plays, and other social events. Very little of their liberty was spent isolated or alone. They took considerable time learning about the curricula of M5's major educational facilities, to which they will someday return at the head of a class of ascenders.

It was here that Kala and Saro experienced the reality of that unforgettable declaration by a Brilliant Evening Star, *"The entire universe is one vast school."* (37:6.2)

Saro recalled and read another statement by the Evening Star, this one on the value and purpose of universal education. She said in part:

"The mortal-survival plan has a practical and serviceable

objective; you are not the recipients of all this divine labor and painstaking training only that you may survive just to enjoy endless bliss and eternal ease. There is a goal of transcendent service concealed beyond the horizon of the present universe age. If the Gods designed merely to take you on one long and eternal joy excursion, they certainly would not so largely turn the whole universe into one vast and intricate practical training school, requisition a substantial part of the celestial creation as teachers and instructors, and then spend ages upon ages piloting you, one by one, through this gigantic universe school of experiential training. The furtherance of the scheme of mortal progression seems to be one of the chief businesses of the present organized universe, and the majority of innumerable orders of created intelligences are either directly or indirectly engaged in advancing some phase of this progressive perfection plan." (48:8.3)

Days six to ten of their M5 liberty they spent on T5. At its central temple, the pair experienced a most pleasurable and extended worship experience. They communed alongside, and along with, high born Sons from Paradise and ascenders like themselves. So intrigued were they with the Sons' worlds that the pair decided to tour all seven of its sub-satellites, to meet as many of those spheres' residents as they could.

Since each of T5's sub-satellites house a single order of sonship, this gave them a much clearer and broader picture of the nature and character of each order, including the Trinitized Sons; all of whom have pledged themselves to eternal service living, teaching and spreading God's truth, beauty and goodness across all time and space.

Saro and Kala learned a great deal in their brief excursions on M5 and T5. While at this fifth level of Mansonia they came to know, befriend, and appreciate a variety of the two spheres' residents. They also made a concerted effort to continue building their universe and superuniverse vocabulary, with Solonia's excellent instruction. At the same time, and through frequent worship, they became ever more intimate with their

Indwellers, Michael, the Divine Minister, and their Guardians.

Each day the pair noted their quickened spirit was uniting with God's, with each other, and with the cosmos on deeper and deeper levels, levels which they heretofore could not have imagined. The pair pledged to return to M5 and T5 with a class of pilgrim ascenders, and again worship with the Sons of God at their consecrated temples of Fatherly adoration.

Right after the three deseraphimed on M6, Kala and Saro received the fifth adjustment, and their four Guardian Angels appeared. The Guardians wanted to welcome them formally and personally invite them to worship on T6, their home world in the System, the World of the Spirit. T6 is a gathering place for the high personalities of the Infinite Spirit and the Divine Minister, whose presence and ministry are everywhere.

In planning their liberty on level six, they decided without debate to accept their Guardians' invitation to worship on T6. And while visiting it, they wanted to touch down on each of T6's seven sub-satellites where individual angelic orders abide.

Saro said, "Solonia, as I recall M6 is where ascenders start training and working in administrative service."

"Yes. And that is mentioned on our tours. We tell arriving ascenders:

"Sojourners on this sphere are permitted to visit transition world number six, where they learn more about the high spirits of the superuniverse, although they are not able to visualize many of these celestial beings. Here they also receive their first lessons in the prospective spirit career which so immediately follows graduation from the morontia training of the local universe." (47:8.1)

"The assistant System Sovereign makes frequent visits to this world, and the initial instruction is here begun in the technique of universe administration. The first lessons embracing the affairs of a whole universe are now imparted." (47:8.2)

"During the sojourn on world number six the mansion world

students achieve a status which is comparable with the exalted development characterizing those evolutionary worlds which have normally progressed beyond the initial stage of light and life. The organization of society on this mansonia is of a high order. The shadow of the mortal nature grows less and less as these worlds are ascended one by one. You are becoming more and more adorable as you leave behind the coarse vestiges of planetary animal origin." (47:8.7)

After considering their many options, and since there was so much they wanted to do, Kala and Saro chose to stay an additional ten days at the sixth level. It was decided that they would spend the first ten on M6 and the last ten on T6. Solonia escorted the pair to their temporary residence in the Melchizedek sector, and departed to file their amended plan at M6 headquarters.

While on M6, the pair associated with various angels and other types of beings who were now coming into their improved spirit vision. They also discovered the roots of a culture of fusion on M6. By the time certain progressive ascenders reach this sphere they are fully prepared to unite with their Indwellers.

Observing M6's residents, Kala and Saro did in fact note the near total absence of the vestiges of animal origin. Most aberrations and gross imperfections they observed in ascendant beings on the lower mansions were not observable here. Those who have ascended this high have passed the tests and completed the training that brings out one's real self, one's true character.

Saro was reminded of this line, *"Coming up through great tribulation' serves to make glorified mortals very kind and understanding, very sympathetic and tolerant."* (47:8.7)

It was on this world, on the way to one of Solonia's favorite places to dine, that she crossed paths with an old friend, a beautiful Seconaphim. She introduced the pair. Kala and Saro were very much charmed by her and quickly extended an invitation to join them for dinner.

As the four sat in a lovely little restaurant on a canal, not far from the sphere's central temple, Saro said, "I recall, there are three kinds of Seconaphim, and each of those three has seven specialties. You all took origin in the Seven Reflective Spirits."

"That is correct," Solonia translated her friend's words. "I am an Import of Time."

Kala asked, "Where are you serving now? What exactly is it that you do?"

"Anywhere I am needed in the System. And my service involves instructing ascenders in both the positive and the negative use of time — work and rest. I am also called on to bear witness before the courts of the Ancients of Days, as to whether time has been well-used or squandered. And the authorities of time and space come to us to project and predict future trends and events."

After an enjoyable exchange among the four of them, and as they were about to part, the Seconaphim said in an endearing, genteel manner, "Solonia informs me you two are tried and true experts in the use of time, and that you have chosen a path of leadership. I predict you will be successful in that endeavor. And that we will, at some point in the near future, meet again here in Mansonia and serve side by side in your chosen work."

While on T6 their Guardians led them on tours of angelically designed temples, residences, universities, and workshops. Kala and Saro were fascinated by the unique beauty, the intriguing subtleties, and the many intricacies of angelic life and social service. It was their time on T6 where the pair came to know and better understand Guardian Angels, and a variety of other types of angelic beings who all take origin in the Third Source and Center, the Infinite Spirit.

Saro's curiosity about his Guardians led him to ask, "How do you spend time when you're off duty? We know one or both of you is always on duty, watching and caring for us. But what else interests you; what do you do in your leisure time?"

"We, like you, have a wide variety of interests, in music, art, the pursuit of perfection, but of a more spiritual nature, of which you are now becoming aware. Aside from your watch-care, we all four attend the extension schools for evolving seraphim, long ago established in the mansion world training regime. We are all in school, aren't we."

Kala recalled and read to Saro this quote about her beautiful Guardians, one she often pondered while on Urantia, longing to know them better.

"Before leaving the mansion worlds, all mortals will have permanent seraphic associates or guardians. And as you ascend the morontia spheres, eventually it is the seraphic guardians who witness and certify the decrees of your eternal union with the Thought Adjusters. Together they have established your personality identities as children of the flesh from the worlds of time. Then, with your attainment of the mature morontia estate, they accompany you through Jerusem and the associated worlds of system progress and culture. After that they go with you to Edentia and its seventy spheres of advanced socialization, and subsequently will they pilot you to the Melchizedeks and follow you through the superb career of the universe headquarters worlds. And when you have learned the wisdom and culture of the Melchizedeks, they will take you on to Salvington, where you will stand face to face with the Sovereign of all Nebadon. And still will these seraphic guides follow you through the minor and major sectors of the superuniverse and on to the receiving worlds of Uversa, remaining with you until you finally enseconaphim for the long Havona flight." (113:7.4)

Their Guardians took over Solonia's duties as escort while they traveled on T6 and its sub-satellites. But she chose to go along with them. First they were led to T6's central temple for a memorable worship among millions of angels of diverse orders. The pair noted that worshiping with Angels has a special flavor of utter and complete submission to divine love. Indwelt as the pair is by God's presence only helped in this internal act of worshipful submission, one which the angels have a talent for both doing and teaching.

Their experiences on T6 and its satellites became invaluable and treasured memories of time spent observing and worshiping with these mind ministers, these loyal, amazing, angelic associates and helpers of ascenders and descenders.

Solonia especially enjoyed the T6 visit, as she relished communing with so many fellow sisters of the same origin, and among her Adjustered friends and their Guardians.

By the time Kala and Saro reached the seventh mansion world, after scores of worship sessions, after meeting hundreds of diverse entities — from fellow pilgrims to fused beings like Andon and Fonta — and after repeated inner revelatory experiences with their Indwellers, they had little else on their minds but uniting with their betrothed.

Following their sixth body/mind adjustment, registering, and settling in, Solonia helped them choose how best to schedule their M7 liberty. It was decided right away — since this would be their final step up the mansion ladder — to extend their liberty by two increments, giving them a full thirty days on M7 and T7.

They decided to explore M7 first, for ten days, beginning with an overhead view on the backs of the mighty passenger birds. During that flight they quickly came to realize M7 is the most complex and highly developed of the mansions. On the ground they discovered it also has the greatest diversity of beings in residence and visiting; that it is the final staging ground for the acme of mansion life, citizenship on Jerusem.

In the pod on the way to the bird launch Solonia offered the pair the excursion guides' insights for ascenders to M7's high culture and refined training:

"The experience on this sphere is the crowning achievement of the immediate post-mortal career. Any discernible differences between those mortals hailing from the

isolated and retarded worlds and those survivors from the more advanced and enlightened spheres are virtually obliterated during the sojourn on the seventh mansion world. Here you will be purged of all the remnants of unfortunate heredity, unwholesome environment, and unspiritual planetary tendencies. The last remnants of the "mark of the beast" are here eradicated. (47:9.1)

"While sojourning on mansonia number seven, permission is granted to visit transition world number seven, the world of the Universal Father. Here you begin a new and more spiritual worship of the unseen Father, a habit you will increasingly pursue all the way up through your long ascending career." (47:9.2)

Saro asked Solonia, "T7 is where the rebels are imprisoned; correct?"

"It is T7's seven satellites where they are detained."

"Have you been to any of the prison worlds?" Kala asked.

"I have been to all many times. It is, by necessity, a duty of escort companions. But no one has gone there to minister to the rebels since Michael's bestowal on Urantia."

After a moment, Saro asked Solonia, "Do you recommend that we visit?"

"I recommend you visit T7, go to the Father's great temple of light and pray about it."

"Solonia, did you join the rebellion?" Kala inquired softly and sincerely.

"We all looked. His words and his presence were so charming it was difficult to believe the rebel leader could be that completely and utterly wrong. But I never took his manifesto seriously. God's benign and benevolent sovereignty over us is obvious to me. And where did the rebels derive their power, even their bodies and minds? Were they self-bestowed? No, I did not succumb to the rebel sophistry, but I have siblings who still have not recanted or repented, and who may perish when the final adjudication of the rebels comes down from the courts of the Ancients of Days.

"Except on the prison spheres, all appetite for rebellion and evil has disappeared from the System. And everyone knows it is futile to try to persuade the few remaining stubborn rebels. Now they are set to give up life rather than abandon their mad belligerence and hostility toward our Creator Son and the heavenly Father. The rebellion was a terrible time for the whole System. Many teachers and their students went over to the rebel cause. And it is not yet finished. The lingering effects still wash over some of the evolutionary worlds which of course creates more grief and confusion for ascenders, and more work and strain for Mansonia's stationary personnel. None of us looks back on it fondly." Solonia shed a tear.

Kala and Saro thoroughly enjoyed the ten days touring M7, always with Solonia at their side offering cultural insights and historical background. It was gratifying and highly educational to meet and converse with so many ascenders who had made their way to the highest of the mansion worlds over many years, and who now look and act the part of enlightened children of God. Indeed, they stand on the very precipice of eternity, as Saro and Kala now do.

Also during those ten days on M7 the pair met with school administrators and educators with whom they might one day work on their return voyage. Here they were introduced to many of the higher methods and more refined tools of teaching that characterize the System's final stage of mansion world schooling and mortal rehabilitation.

And it was here that they encountered a group of Paradise Finaliters touring the mansions on the way to T1, their residential world in the System. These are beings who long ago fused, ascended to and were embraced by God on Paradise, then returned to their universe of origin for the edification and encouragement of newly ascended pilgrims, ones like Saro and Kala just now beginning the Paradise journey.

With the aid of energy transformers the Finaliters were made visible to Kala's and Saro's eyes; filling them with cosmic amazement and spirit joy. Observing these perfected beings who have graduated from the highest universities of the Grand Universe, ones who have met and been embraced by God on Paradise, does indeed inspire all less experienced beings who chance to 'see' and be taught by them.

After that encounter, they decided to enroll in a three-day symposium on Paradise ascension led by none other than these Finaliters touring M7. Kala and Saro were mightily thrilled by seeing and hearing about the experiences of these perfected graduates of time and space, these beings who are invisible and normally out of reach. From them the pair received a vastly expanded concept of the Paradise climb, Paradise culture, and Paradise worship.

Days eleven through twenty they set aside to tour T7 and perhaps its associated satellites, the detention spheres. Days twenty-one to thirty, they chose to keep open for the time being.

~ Chapter 19 ~
The Father's World, The Prison Worlds, Call to Fuse

During their extended seventh level liberty, the pair received their seventh and eighth body/mind adjustments. Looking back, they could see, with each adjustment, a growing ability to discern a wider variety of beings, to reach ever deeper levels of worship, to broaden the meaning and value of every sense, sight and sound, and to learn more easily. Morontia vision was expanding, their souls were well nigh bursting with the joy of intimacy and oneness with their Indwellers. All the challenges, experiences, acquired wisdom, and spiritual values of lives well-lived were now culminating on M7. Kala and Saro were feeling closer and closer to God, Michael, and the Divine Mother, with each day's passing.

At the end of ten days on M7, the trio enseraphimed to go visit the World of the Father. T7 is very different from the other six, in that no one lives there. It is known as the 'silent sphere of the System.' Worshipers from all of the System's worlds commune with the Universal Father in T7's great temple of light. It is the only activity on this quiet world whereon no residents may be found, only a minimal staff to maintain the Father's temple and see to His guests.

Kala and Saro were immediately and divinely captivated by the power of the connection they felt on the Father's world. Being indwelt by fragments of the Universal Father created a natural resonance during their most beautiful, fulfilling, and transcendent worship yet. So enraptured were they by worship on this sphere that very soon time and space merged in the moment creating the sensation and the reality of the ultimate unity of all things and beings. Divine attunement was approaching the highest levels possible at this juncture in their eventful journey.

Solonia remained with them, enjoying the heightened pleasure of worship in this rarified divine ambiance. The quality of worship on T7 also seemed to be improved by the many types of high beings in attendance. As worshipers flowed on and off the sphere, in and out of the great temple, all appeared to share the same feeling of joy in the intimate knowledge of being a personally loved and divinely adored child of God. So intense, intriguing, and compelling was their worship that before the pair realized it, the day had passed, during which they absorbed many new, vivid, and unimagined insights into the nature and character of their indwelling God fragment, the Great God of Paradise, the Father of all.

As the light began to fade the trio left the central temple to discuss Saro's and Kala's plans for the remaining nine days. They took stairs to a high promenade that offered a view of the magnificent temple of light below. They were enthralled by the transcendent beauty of it. No word was spoken for a long while.

Finally Kala said to Solonia, "Thank you for staying with us all day." She squeezed her hand in sincere appreciation, then asked Saro, "How do you feel about remaining here?"

"I was about to suggest it," he replied. "Solonia, would you like to return to M7?"

"Yes, but please contact me before you leave here."

After transportation arrived, the trio embraced and Solonia departed.

"I don't feel hungry or tired. You?" Saro asked.

"My love, all I feel is the urge to return to the temple."

The pair stayed almost two days on the Father's world, remaining in worship mode, taking only water, air, and God's good love. They enjoyed each session supremely and felt no hunger or other need. And during each session their Paradise

Partners revealed more insights and greater cosmic perspectives. An astonishing variety of additional information and insight was conveyed while they communed within on T7. Very much of it pertained to their Adjusters' extensive and invaluable experiences indwelling others, for whom Kala and Saro were now feeling immensely grateful.

Between worship sessions they walked around the great temple on the encircling promenade, sometimes alone, sometimes together, and sometimes with a group of other stalwart worshippers. Finally the urge to worship subsided and they knew it was time to return to M7 and reconnect with the residential world. Before enseraphiming for the short flight to M7 they contacted Solonia to arrange their meeting time and place.

She joined the pair for a meal upon their return. While eating the trio discussed their individual experiences worshiping on T7. Kala and Saro tried to express how much they enjoyed the pure, unbroken, shared adoration between God and child; and the depth of the insights they received. They attempted to describe how beautiful it was hearing music of the realms, and seeing enlarged picturizations of the cosmos from the exalted perspective of their beloved Indwellers. And how the worship experience had continuously expanded over the two days.

After listening to their descriptions, Solonia said, "In worship I relate to the Father, but through the Mother, they are one, of course."

"Solonia, have you ever wanted, or wondered what it would be like, to host an Adjuster?" Saro asked.

"We see and live with Adjustered ones everyday, so naturally some have on occasion speculated about it because of the remarkable attributes, creative potentials, and inspiring values we observe in you morontia progressors, you with so little cosmic experience. But, perhaps, we wonder about being Adjustered no more than ones like you wonder what being a non-ascending Morontia Companion is like. That said, only the

Gods know their creatures from the inside. Which reminds me, you two are certified as having attained the first psychic circle.

The news came during your days within the Father's bosom on T7."

Saro and Kala were not surprised. They had already realized it from the inside, so close and intimate were they with, and in, God. Their worship experience on T7 felt as if it was a final stride of their inward journey to oneness with the Divine Indweller.

The trio then debated Kala's and Saro's next step of their outward journey, whether to tour the seven prison worlds that surround T7. Solonia asked them, "What was the answer to your prayers?"

They glanced at each other and replied at the same time, "Yes."

As soon as they landed on the first prison world, Kala and Saro sensed a certain and definite bleakness. No one except the transport angels and support personnel were present. Solonia led them outside the walls of the spaceport for a wider view. They appeared to be alone. No activity was apparent.

"Are we the only visitors?" Kala asked.

"At the moment, yes," replied Solonia.

Saro speculated, "Maybe the inmates are all asleep?"

"No. They know we are here. But they will not come forward to greet Adjustered ones," replied Solonia.

The pair pondered that a moment and Kala asked, "Because they know we can't be swayed?"

"That is correct."

"Solonia, you knew this and chose not to tell us beforehand," said Saro, "because you felt we require first-hand experience?"

"Yes."

It took another moment for that to sink in. Kala thought to

ask, "Will it be the same on the other six prison worlds?"

"We do not know that for a certainty," Solonia replied.

"So, you're thinking we should visit each one?" asked Saro.

"It is the only way you will know with absolute surety, and for all eternity."

Kala and Saro thought about it and agreed there was nothing to fear and perhaps something to learn, and thereby elected to proceed to the second detention sphere. But the non-reception and apparent vacancy there was the same as on the first. They went on to the third, then the fourth, and the fifth, and finally, on the sixth prison sphere they were greeted, in a manner.

Solonia looked them in the eye and said in complete sincerity, "Kala, Saro, meet the leader of Nebadon's third rebellion."

The pair could hardly believe their hearing at first. But they, through Adjuster, Spirit of Truth, and Guardian connection, sensed it was so. And they noted his brilliant appearance.

Neither Kala nor Saro felt compelled to speak, so they didn't. In fact, there was nothing to say. He had chosen his path, and they theirs. And neither in any way, or fashion, coincides.

Suddenly, feelings of pity came to Kala and Saro. At that instant the figure turned dark and moved away.

"He never fails to try, even with Adjustered ones," Solonia lamented. At that moment, Kala and Saro realized they had just encountered a high-born and brilliant being who is willfully and cosmically insane.

With no one else to greet them, Solonia asked, "On to prison world 7?"

But the seventh world also sent no one to greet its visitors. The pair found it as bleak, pitiable, and forlorn as the others. They decided to return to the Father's World.

Kala and Saro once more communed within on this silent

world, with Solonia close by. But, after only a few moments, a clear and distinct voice was heard. The message was unmistakable, "Our time has come."

Their eyes opened, they looked at each other, then at Solonia. Evidently she hadn't heard, as she was still in worship mode. Kala and Saro knew immediately what this meant. They stood up and led Solonia out of the temple toward the seraphic launch.

As they left, Solonia asked, "Did you receive instructions?"

The pair stopped and faced her. Kala answered, "We did. We're returning to M7." Solonia then fully realized it was near time for her wards, her ascending friends, to unite with their Adjusters.

No sooner had they landed on M7 than their Guardians delivered the news. One of Kala's angels said, "You have been granted citizenship on Jerusem. And you are instructed to proceed to its fusion temple forthwith."

The pair smiled knowingly. Then the six of them embraced as Solonia looked on with adoration and admiration. Their Guardians expressed delight and pleasure at the pair's success, and the assurance that they too will be certified for the Paradise journey when Kala and Saro are joined to God. They and their wards are about to take the first step that will ensure them a role in the eternal unfolding of divine plans and endless existence serving as children of God.

Solonia immediately filed a new itinerary, routing them to Jerusem the next morning. The last day on M7 they spent visiting several of its temples and coming to know some of the diverse beings they were now able to see, thanks to the eight adjustments, and their brief and fascinating odyssey sailing up to Mansonia's headwaters.

The pair ended the day with a last supper reenactment at their temporary lodging, just between them, followed by a wakeful night under M7's beautiful sky communing within and giving thanks for the now imminent possibility of entering into eternal life and enjoying the fullness of true spiritual liberty in the Universe of universes.

They found a nook in which to recline and observe the stars. "Have you thought about what fusion will be like?" Saro asked.

Kala thought a moment, "The only thing that comes to mind, is spiritual climax."

He laughed and said, "Yes, life is essentially romancing the Divine...so much is ahead of us, Kala. But it feels good now to know our ultimate destiny and have a glimpse of the beautiful path to it, doesn't it?!"

"It does," she whispered. They then, once more, slipped into intimate worship of God, one who is most worthy of it.

Just before dawn, Kala spoke prophetic words to her beloved Saro, "Eternity begins in earnest today. For two more of God's children from Urantia." She caressed his face and kissed him.

After landing on Jerusem, Solonia took them directly to the morontia temple complex where the fusion process takes place and entered their names into both the official registry of System citizens, and the log of that day's fusion candidates. The temple was the grandest Kala and Saro had yet seen. Its beauty and allure, the creative employment of light and materials, the wonderful works of art and sculpture, the Celestial Artisans' use of, "almost all of the two hundred morontia elements," according to Solonia, deeply impressed the pair. It seemed a fitting place for such a profound and catalytic transmutation of material energy and divine spirit.

The temple is surrounded by immense residential areas constructed especially to house off-sphere visitors, local students, and Jerusem citizens attending the fusion ceremony. At the center of the huge temple's circular promenade is a spacious stage on and above which fusion occurs.

Looking at the manifest Solonia said, "You have over twelve thousand co-fusers. But you will be separated into groups of one thousand."

Saro asked, "May we be in the same group?"

"You may. It has been arranged."

While preparations were being made for this once-in-an-eternal-career event, the trio walked around the temple's seven circular galleries, and spoke with many fellow fusion candidates and their friends. They learned that most had ascended from an evolutionary world; had originated in some order of animal being with one, two, or three brains; were breathers and non-breathers. Almost all had acquired an Adjuster in mortal life, died, and progressed up the mansion regime within a large class. A class not unlike the one Kala and Saro will lead after forming and training their team. But first, the business at hand, ending the period of betrothal with their Indwellers by wedding themselves to God in Eternity.

When all was set, when careful preparations were completed, an emeritus leader of the System's Morontia Companions took the stage. She introduced a Mighty Messenger, a former mortal who has passed all the great tests, completed the long training of time and space in the seven superuniverses, traversed Havona's billion worlds, and has met and embraced God on Paradise. The Messenger is a onetime Nebadon citizen who was Trinitized and is now a member of the Paradise Finaliter's Corps. Kala and Saro more than once thought of pursuing such a path as these 'mighty' universal servers.

He stepped forward to address this happy group of millions — and millions more viewing remotely. With a beaming smile he said, "Welcome to all." A roar of cheers rolled over the immense crowd and resounded off the promenade walls.

"Mighty Messengers, in common with all Trinity-embraced sons, are assigned to all phases of superuniverse activities. They maintain constant connection with their headquarters through the superuniverse reflectivity service. Mighty Messengers serve in all sectors of a superuniverse and frequently execute missions to the local universes and even to the individual worlds. (22:2.7)

"The sending of Adjusters, their indwelling, is indeed one of the unfathomable mysteries of God the Father. These fragments of the divine nature of the Universal Father carry with them the potential of creature immortality. Adjusters are immortal spirits, and union with them confers eternal life upon the soul of the fused mortal. (40:7.1)

"These indwelling fragments of God are with your order of being from the early days of physical existence through all of the ascending career in Nebadon and Orvonton and on through Havona, even to Paradise itself. Thereafter, in the eternal adventure, this same Adjuster is one with you and of you. (40:7.3)

"The spirits of mortal fusion always ascend to the level of origin; such spirit entities unfailingly return to the sphere of primal source. (40:10.1)

"The Thought Adjuster, hailing from the Father on Paradise, never stops until the mortal son stands face to face with the eternal God. (40:10.2)

"Adjuster-fused ascenders do indeed have a grand and glorious career as finaliters spread out before them in the eternal future. Adjuster-fused mortals are destined to penetrate the universe of universes. (40:10.5)

"When the evolving soul and the divine Adjuster are finally and eternally fused, each gains all of the experiencible qualities of the other. This co-ordinate personality possesses all of the experiential memory of survival once held by the ancestral mortal mind and then resident in the morontia soul, and in addition thereto this potential finaliter embraces all the experiential memory of the Adjuster throughout the mortal indwellings of all time. But it will require an eternity of the future for an Adjuster ever completely to endow the personality partnership with the meanings and values which the divine Monitor carries forward from the eternity of the past. (110:7.5)

"Thought Adjuster fusion imparts eternal actualities to personality which were previously only potential. Among these new endowments may be mentioned: fixation of divinity quality,

past-eternity experience and memory, immortality, and a phase of qualified potential absoluteness. (112:7.1)

"When fusion with the Adjuster has been effected, there can be no future danger to the eternal career of such a personality. (112:7.4)

"When the self attains the spiritual level, it has become a secure value in the universe, and this new value is predicated upon the fact that survival decisions have been made, which fact has been witnessed by eternal fusion with the Thought Adjuster. (112:7.6)

"This extraordinary partnership is one of the most engrossing and amazing of all the cosmic phenomena of this universe age. (112:7.11)

"With Adjuster fusion the Universal Father has completed his promise of the gift of himself to his material creatures; he has fulfilled the promise, and consummated the plan, of the eternal bestowal of divinity upon humanity. Now begins the human attempt to realize and to actualize the limitless possibilities that are inherent in the supernal partnership with God which has thus factualized. (112:7.14)

"The present known destiny of surviving mortals is the Paradise Corps of the Finality; this is also the goal of destiny for all Thought Adjusters who become joined in eternal union with their mortal companions. At present the Paradise finaliters are working throughout the grand universe in many undertakings, but we all conjecture that they will have other and even more supernal tasks to perform in the distant future after the seven superuniverses have become settled in light and life, and when the finite God has finally emerged from the mystery which now surrounds this Supreme Deity. (112:7.15)

"What an adventure! What a romance! A gigantic creation to be administered by the children of the Supreme, these personalized and humanized Adjusters, these Adjusterized and eternalized mortals, these mysterious combinations and eternal associations of the highest known manifestation of the essence of the First Source and Center and the lowest form of intelligent

life capable of comprehending and attaining the Universal Father." (112:7.18)

He then offered congratulations to the group of near-fusers now fully prepared and longing for the satisfaction of the consummation of a union with their indwelling fragments of divine essence. Today is a day of affirmation, confirmation, and reward for embracing divine love, giving unflinching faith, and manifesting unshakable loyalty. Today is the day twelve thousand more children of God, daughters and sons of Nebadon, will be born into eternal life.

~ Chapter 20 ~
Fusion, New Beginning

At that point the Archangel of Records and the Supervising Archangel were summoned to the stage. The Archangel of Record said, "And now, you begin life anew." The pair had learned enough of the System language to understand without Solonia's translation.

After those few words of initiation she instructed fusion candidates to assemble at a designated holding area not far from, and connected to, the stage's center. It took some time for all candidates to gather and find their group. They were assigned to twelve groups of one thousand each, plus one of nearly two hundred. Kala and Saro were informed, when the time came, their group would take the stage first. Meanwhile the vast on-looking audience took seats and prepared themselves for celestial fireworks.

As they waited and watched, Saro recalled a quote he had often pondered while on Urantia, about this moment before fusion. He recited part of it for Kala.

"...what a beautiful occasion when mortals thus forgather to witness the ascension of their loved ones in spiritual flames, and what a contrast to those earlier ages when mortals must commit their dead to the embrace of the terrestrial elements! The scenes of weeping and wailing characteristic of earlier epochs of human evolution are now replaced by ecstatic joy and the sublimest enthusiasm..." (55:2.5)

Before they were asked to move to the appointed place at center stage, the thirteen groups watched as a host of beautifully arrayed celestial personalities formed a wide ring, positioning themselves between the stage and the audience. These personalities possess the ability to protect observers from the tremendous energies released at the instant the "life flash" occurs.

Kala and Saro felt supremely peaceful. They were thoroughly enjoying the unspoken camaraderie and spiritual buoyancy of the occasion, along with the rest of their group of fellow fusers, and in view of billions of enthusiastic observers.

With everything and everyone in readiness, the Archangel asked that all well-wishing friends and relations remove themselves from the groups. Kala and Saro turned to Solonia and expressed wordless appreciation and beaming love with a memorable embrace. The three all shed a tear of ineffable joy and thanksgiving for each other and this moment.

"When will we see you again?" Kala asked.

"I have requested — and been granted — permission to remain at your side, to be your lieutenant in your coming labors, receiving and training a class of your fellow Urantians — if you want me. But I am leaving you for the moment, I love you."

"We want you!" the pair said as one.

But before they could ask where she was going, Solonia departed and their four Guardians appeared, simultaneous with the greatest Adjuster awareness they had so far experienced. It suddenly became a supreme moment. The Supervising Archangel confirmed that the first group of one thousand were prepared. She directed that they proceed to the fusion arena, center stage. The Guardians congratulated the pair and the six of them embraced. Kala and Saro strongly felt their angelic joy. When the first fusion group received its final call their four Guardians left bearing broad and beautiful smiles. When they were on stage and in the proper position, the Archangel of Records came before this group of now supremely conscious fusion candidates to offer a final address in prayer, as the attentive audience genuflected and listened.

"Father, today we gather to witness the creation of 12,192 new beings whose predecessors, in cooperation with your divine fragments, have made the final and irrevocable choice to become your child for all eternity. They have done this of their own accord, compelled only by the gravity your unfailing love and the infinite power of your extended grace and bounteous mercy. We thank you for this extension of divine love, and for them.

"The Adjustered children who become Finaliters and serve in the evolving universes of time and space provide us with inspiration to better know you, and more opportunity to serve you, thereby assisting in your great and immediate work of unifying the Grand Universe in light and life, thus creating even greater service opportunities for us all in the ages to come, and in universes not yet inhabited.

"As we witness the fusion of ascending pilgrims of time with divine descenders from eternity, we are humbled by your marvelous and stupendous plan that gives each and every being an enduring role in the age-long realization of the Supreme Being. We thank you for your solicitous watch-care that forgets none and cares for all. We know that your truth, beauty, and goodness are glorified and expanded in these children who have elected to follow our sovereign Creator Son, our divine parent Michael, who is the Way, the Truth, and the Life for all Nebadon's children."

She then stepped off the stage and a great quiet came over this group of billions. They were, everyone, now focused entirely on the one thousand beings about to make a cosmic leap into eternal life.

After a moment of tingling silence, the thousand candidates heard the same voice. Only they and the attending Archangels heard the voice declare, "This is a beloved child in whom I am well pleased." These few words indicate that ascenders are about to cross the threshold of eternity.

Kala and Saro suddenly felt weightless and began rising very slowly. As the group rose together, the area around them began to vibrate with sound and emanate light. They took a last look at reality through dual eyes. Gradually they ascended, moving faster and faster. The on-looking audience began to cheer, watching the morontia bodies rapidly turning to brilliant light. Beautiful and resounding cosmic laughter was the last sounds heard from the ascenders.

The now luminous group was quickly accelerated high in the air until a critical point was reached. Suddenly great and blinding flashes burst forth followed by a dazzling array of one thousand shafts of rainbow lights splintering in every direction, then merging and filling the whole of the Jerusem sky, culminating as one great unified light of divine sparkle and perfect hue. The audience cheered and spontaneously wept for joy, and for the glory of our omnipotent God who makes the seemingly miraculous possible, the joining of the creatures of time and space with the Creator of eternity and infinity, and before their very eyes.

The pair next found themselves in renewed morontia form at a nearly deserted Resurrection Hall on M1. They were greeted by their four Guardian Angels and Solonia, who took them immediately to their original Mansonia residence. How refreshing to see again the lovely, simple cottage with the swinging platform that hangs from the huge flowering tree in back, next to the park where they spent their first night on M1. It was under that tree where they first met Solonia. And it was here where they first connected with their Adjusters as newly resurrected pilgrims many days ago — many days that now seemed to them like a lifetime unto itself.

After arriving and re-examining their charming little abode, the group went out back to commune under the great tree's falling petals. Before they all mounted the swing, they embraced in a circle. The seven held together as one for a transcendent moment. It was a beautiful and touching scene as they embraced in out-going and selfless love, while the aromatic petals drifted down and over them. After a while of unspoken joy and shared affection, their Guardians informed the pair of their new names. The names by which they shall forever be known.

Solonia liked them very much, exclaiming, "Perfect!!"

With deep love and affection one of Kala's Guardians said to the pair, "We now have much in common."

All newly fused beings are granted forty days liberty. The first twenty the pair spent touring worlds of the System they had not previously visited, meeting the residents and learning about the local culture, also communing within at selected temples where fused and non-fused ascenders foregather.

They also took time to consider the grander options that now came before them as a result of fusion. Specifically their eventual destiny, their route home to God on Paradise, including the possibility of pursuing careers as Mighty Messengers. But since their immediate project of leading a class of ex-Urantians up through Mansonia training will require an extended stay in the System, they chose to postpone most of those decisions, thinking their selections may be even wiser at the end of their long tenures as class leaders.

The second twenty days the pair used to become more familiar with the physical, intellectual, and spiritual facilities on all the worlds of the System. They especially sought out educational tools that had proven effective for other educators and leaders. In their customary selfless fashion, true to the beauty and depth of their character, they wanted to begin at once assimilating knowledge and creating worthy plans for their coming service as leaders of a class of their fellows. What an honor to lead a group of Urantian siblings up and through the seven heavens of Mansonia, and on to Jerusem, where one cycle of spirit training ends and a new one begins. For this dedicated pair, now of Adjuster-fused status, this felt like the real beginning of an eternal friendship, the start of an infinite voyage with God, the maker and keeper of all beings and things, even our Universal Father.

*When your earthly course
in temporary form has been run,
you are to awaken
on the shores of a better world,
and eventually you will be united
with your faithful Adjuster
in an eternal embrace.
And this fusion constitutes the mystery
of making God and man one,
the mystery of finite creature evolution,
but it is eternally true.*
112:7.2 (1237.4)

INDEX OF QUOTES
from
The URANTIA Book

Quote location format:

Paper:Section.Paragraph (page number.paragraph)

Page 14 ~ "In commemoration of the mortal transit of Jesus of Nazareth on Urantia." 188:3.11 (2015.7)

Page 17 ~ ...the act of worship becomes increasingly all-encompassing until it eventually attains the glory of the highest experiential delight and the most exquisite pleasure known to created beings. 27:7.1 (303.5)

Page 20 ~ Paul learned of the existence of the morontia worlds and of the reality of morontia materials, for he wrote, "They have in heaven a better and more enduring substance. 48:1.7 (542.4)

Page 27 ~ Human things must be known in order to be loved, but divine things must be loved in order to be known. 102:1.1 (1118.4) [Quoting Blaise Pascal.]

Page 62 ~ Permit me to quote an Archangel who very wisely stated: 'To material beings the spirit world is more or less unreal; to spirit beings the material world is almost entirely unreal, being merely a shadow of the substance of spirit realities.' 44:0.15 (498.6)

Page 62 ~ And always, as you ascend upward on the scale of life, will you retain the ability to recognize and fraternize with the fellow beings of previous and lower levels of existence. Each new translation or resurrection will add one more group of spirit beings to your vision range without in the least depriving you of the ability to recognize your friends and fellows of former estates. 44:0.18 (498.9)

Page 64 ~ "The methods employed in many of the higher schools are beyond the human concept of the art of teaching truth, but this is the keynote of the whole educational system: character acquired by enlightened experience. The teachers provide the enlightenment; the universe station and the ascender's status afford the opportunity for experience; the wise utilization of these two augments character. 37:6.3 (412.3)

Page 64 ~ "Fundamentally, the Nebadon educational system provides for your assignment to a task and then affords you opportunity to receive instruction as to the ideal and divine method of best performing that task. You are given a definite task to perform, and at the same time you are provided with teachers who are qualified to instruct you in the best method of executing your assignment. The divine plan of education provides for the intimate association of work and instruction. We teach you how best to execute the things we command you to do. 37:6.4 (412.4)

Page 64 ~ "The purpose of all this training and experience is to prepare you for admission to the higher and more spiritual training spheres of the superuniverse. Progress within a given realm is individual, but transition from one phase to another is usually by classes. 37:6.5 (412.5)

Page 64 ~ "The progression of eternity does not consist solely in spiritual development. Intellectual acquisition is also a part of universal education. The experience of the mind is broadened equally with the expansion of the spiritual horizon. Mind and spirit are afforded like opportunities for training and advancement. But in all this superb training of mind and spirit you are forever free from the handicaps of mortal flesh. No longer must you constantly referee the conflicting contentions of your divergent spiritual and material natures. At last you are qualified to enjoy the unified urge of a glorified mind long since divested of primitive animalistic trends towards things material." 37:6.6 (412.6)

Page 66 ~ ...They are devoted to the care and culture of the material phases of these headquarters worlds, from Jerusem to Salvington. Spornagia are neither spirits nor persons; they are an animal order of existence, but if you could see them, you would agree that they seem to be perfect animals. 37:10.3 (416.3)

Page 66 ~ 'a mechanical nature' 50:3.3 (574.5)

Page 67 ~ "mark of the beast" 47:9.1 (538.6) Also Bible, Rev 16:2, 19:20

Page 67 ~ On the mansion worlds the seraphic evangels will help you to choose wisely among the optional routes to Edentia, Salvington, Uversa, and Havona. If there are a number of equally advisable routes, these will be put before you, and you will be permitted to select the one that most appeals to you. These seraphim then make recommendations to the four and twenty advisers on Jerusem concerning that course which would be most advantageous for each ascending soul. 48:6.5 (552.3)

Page 79 ~ Even when the air currents are ascending, no bird can soar except by outstretched wings. 91:8.9 (1002.1)

Page 87 ~ ... in the morontia life, and increasingly on its higher levels, the personality form will vary directly in accordance with the nature of the inner person. 112:6.3 (1236.1)

Page 94 ~ The Gods are my caretakers; I shall not stray; Side by side they lead me in the beautiful paths and glorious refreshing of life everlasting.

I shall not, in this Divine Presence, want for food nor thirst for water.

Though I go down into the valley of uncertainty or ascend up into the worlds of doubt,

Though I move in loneliness or with the fellows of my kind,

Though I triumph in the choirs of light or falter in the solitary places of the spheres,

Your good spirit shall minister to me, and your glorious angel will comfort me.

Though I descend into the depths of darkness and death itself,

I shall not doubt you nor fear you,

For I know that in the fullness of time and the glory of your name

You will raise me up to sit with you on the battlements on high. 48:6.9 (552.7)

Page 105 ~ The Adjuster, while passive regarding purely temporal welfare, is divinely active concerning all the affairs of your eternal future. 110:1.4 (1204.2)

Page 106 ~ Survivors arriving on this first of the detention spheres present so many and such varied defects of creature character and deficiencies of mortal experience that the major activities of the realm are occupied with the correction and cure of these manifold legacies of the life in the flesh. 47:3.8 (533.6)

Page 107 ~ After attaining the Nebadon Corps of Perfection, Spirit-fused ascenders may accept assignment as Universe Aids, this being one of the avenues of continuing experiential growth which is open to them. Thus do they become candidates for commissions to the high service of interpreting the viewpoints of the evolving creatures of the material worlds to the celestial authorities of the local universe. 37:5.4 (411.2)

Page 110 ~ When enseraphimed, you go to sleep for a specified time, and you will awake at the designated moment. The length of a journey when in transit sleep is immaterial. You are not directly aware of the passing of time. It is as if you went to sleep on a transport vehicle in one city and, after resting in peaceful slumber all night, awakened in another and distant metropolis. You journeyed while you slumbered. And so you take flight through space, enseraphimed, while you rest — sleep. The transit sleep is induced by the liaison between the Adjusters and the seraphic transporters. 39:2.12 (431.1)

Page 113 ~ When celestial beings are to be enseraphimed for transfer from one world to another, they are brought to the headquarters of the sphere and, after due registry, are inducted into the transit sleep. Meantime, the transport seraphim moves into a horizontal position immediately above the universe energy pole of the planet. While the energy shields are wide open, the sleeping personality is skillfully deposited, by the officiating seraphic assistants, directly on top of the transport angel. Then both the upper and lower pairs of shields are carefully closed and adjusted. And now, a strange metamorphosis begins as the seraphim is made ready to swing into the energy currents of the universe circuits. To outward appearance the seraphim grows pointed at both extremities and becomes so enshrouded in an odd light of amber hue that very soon it is impossible to distinguish the enseraphimed personality. When all is in readiness for departure, the chief of transport makes the proper inspection of the carriage of life, carries out the routine tests to ascertain whether or not the angel is properly encircuited, and then announces that the traveler is properly enseraphimed, that the energies are adjusted, that the angel is insulated, and that everything is in readiness for the departing flash. The mechanical controllers, two of them, next take their positions. By this time the transport seraphim has become an almost transparent, vibrating, torpedo-shaped outline of glistening luminosity. Now the transport dispatcher of the realm summons the auxiliary batteries of the living energy transmitters, usually one thousand in number; as he announces the destination of the transport, he reaches out and touches the near point of the seraphic carriage, which shoots forward with lightning-like speed, leaving a trail of celestial luminosity as far as the planetary atmospheric investment extends. 39:5.14 (438.7)

Page 116 ~ The progressive changes result in altered reactions to the morontia environment, such as modifications in food requirements and numerous other personal practices. 48:2.23 (544.6)

Page 117 ~ It is on this sphere that you are more fully inducted into the mansonia life. The groupings of the morontia life begin to take form; working groups and social organizations start to function, communities take on formal proportions, and the advancing mortals inaugurate new social orders and governmental arrangements. 47:4.1 (534.5)

Page 117 ~ As you ascend the mansion worlds one by one, they become more crowded with the morontia activities of advancing survivors. As you go forward, you will recognize more and more of the Jerusem features added to the mansion worlds. The sea of glass makes its appearance on the second mansonia. 47:4.3 (534.7)

Page 117 ~ Mansonia number one is a very material sphere, presenting the early beginnings of the morontia regime. You are still a near human and not far removed from the limited viewpoints of mortal life, but each world discloses definite progress. From sphere to sphere you grow less material, more intellectual, and slightly more spiritual. The spiritual progress is greatest on the last three of these seven progressive worlds. 47:4.6 (535.2)

Page 117 ~ Mansonia number two more specifically provides for the removal of all phases of intellectual conflict and for the cure of all varieties of mental disharmony. The effort to master the significance of morontia mota, begun on the first mansion world, is here more earnestly continued. The development on mansonia number two compares with the intellectual status of the post-Magisterial Son culture of the ideal evolutionary worlds. 47:4.8 (535.4)

Page 126 ~ Mansonia the third is the headquarters of the Mansion World Teachers. Though they function on all seven of the mansion spheres, they maintain their group headquarters at the center of the school circles of world number three. There are millions of these instructors on the mansion and higher morontia worlds. 47:5.1 (535.5)

Page 126 ~ On this sphere more positive educational work is begun. The training of the first two mansion worlds is mostly of a deficiency nature — negative — in that it has to do with supplementing the experience of the life in the flesh. On this third mansion world the survivors really begin their progressive morontia culture. The chief purpose of this training is to enhance the understanding of the correlation of morontia mota and mortal logic, the co-ordination of morontia mota and human philosophy. Surviving mortals now gain practical insight into true metaphysics. This is the real introduction to the intelligent comprehension of cosmic meanings and universe interrelationships. The culture of the third mansion world partakes of the nature of the post-bestowal Son age of a normal inhabited planet." 47:5.3 (536.1)

Page 131 ~ ...Reason is the understanding technique of the sciences; faith is the insight technique of religion; mota is the technique of the morontia level. Mota is a super-material reality sensitivity which is beginning to compensate incomplete growth, having for its substance knowledge-reason and for its essence faith-insight. Mota is a super-philosophical reconciliation of divergent reality perception which is non-attainable by material personalities; it is predicated, in part, on the experience of having survived the material life of the flesh. 103:6.7 (1136.2)

Page 131 ~ ...In the mortal state, nothing can be absolutely proved; both science and religion are predicated on assumptions. On the morontia level, the postulates of both science and religion are capable of partial proof by mota logic. On the spiritual level of maximum status, the need for finite proof gradually vanishes before the actual experience of and with reality; but even then there is much beyond the finite that remains unproved. 103:7.10 (1139.2)

Page 131 ~ Providence becomes increasingly discernible as men reach upward from the material to the spiritual. The attainment of completed spiritual insight enables the ascending personality to detect harmony in what was theretofore chaos. Even morontia mota represents a real advance in this direction. 118:10.19 (1306.8)

Page 133 ~ When you arrive on the fourth mansion world, you have well entered upon the morontia career; you have progressed a long way from the initial material existence. Now are you given permission to make visits to transition world number four, there to become familiar with the headquarters and training schools of the superangels, including the Brilliant Evening Stars. Through the good offices of these superangels of the fourth transition world the morontia visitors are enabled to draw very close to the various orders of the Sons of God during the periodic visits to Jerusem, for new sectors of the system capital are gradually opening up to the advancing mortals as they make these repeated visits to the headquarters world. New grandeurs are progressively unfolding to the expanding minds of these ascenders. 47:6.1 (536.2)

Page 134 ~ On the fourth mansonia the individual ascender more fittingly finds his place in the group working and class functions of the morontia life. Ascenders here develop increased appreciation of the broadcasts and other phases of local universe culture and progress. 47:6.2 (536.3)

Page 134 ~ It is during the period of training on world number four that the ascending mortals are really first introduced to the demands and delights of the true social life of morontia creatures. And it is indeed a new experience for evolutionary creatures to participate in social activities which are predicated neither on personal aggrandizement nor on self-seeking conquest. A new social order is being introduced, one based on the understanding sympathy of mutual appreciation, the unselfish love of mutual service, and the overmastering motivation of the realization of a common and supreme destiny — the Paradise goal of worshipful and divine perfection. Ascenders are all becoming self-conscious of God-knowing, God-revealing, God-seeking, and God-finding. 47:6.3 (536.4)

Page 137 ~ "Not a single Jerusem citizen was lost. Every ascendant mortal survived the fiery trial and emerged from the crucial test triumphant and altogether victorious." 53:7.12 (608.8)

Page 138 ~ Lanaforge, Mansurotia, Sadib, Holdant, Vilton, Fortant, and Hanavard. 45:3.1 (512.1)

Page 138 ~ 'four and twenty elders sitting, clothed in white raiment' 45:4.1 (513.4) Also in the New Testament, Revelations 4, 5, 11, 19.

Page 138 ~ Onagar, Mansant, Onamonalonton, Orlandof, Porshunta, Singlangton, Fantad, Orvonon, Adam, Eve, Enoch, Moses, Elijah, Machiventa Melchizedek, John the Baptist, and a Midwayer named, 1-2-3 the First. 45:4.2 (513.5)

Page 138 ~ The great divisions of celestial life have their headquarters and immense preserves on Jerusem, including the various orders of divine Sons, high spirits, superangels, angels, and midway creatures. The central abode of this wonderful sector is the chief temple of the Material Sons. 45:5.1 (514.12)

Page 139 ~ The probationary nursery itself is supervised by one thousand couples of Material Sons and Daughters, volunteers from the Jerusem colony. 45:6.9 (517.2)

Page 140 ~ Mortal survivors spend much of their leisure on the system capital observing and studying the life habits and conduct of these superior semi-physical sex creatures, for these citizens of Jerusem are the immediate sponsors and mentors of the mortal survivors from the time they attain citizenship on the headquarters world until they take leave for Edentia. 45:6.2 (515.8)

Page 141 ~ Sex experience in a physical sense is past for these ascenders, but in close association with the Material Sons and Daughters, both individually and as members of their families, these sex-deficient mortals are enabled to compensate the social, intellectual, emotional, and spiritual aspects of their deficiency. Thus are all those humans whom circumstances or bad judgment deprived of the benefits of advantageous sex association on the evolutionary worlds, here on the system capitals afforded full opportunity to acquire these essential mortal experiences in close and loving association with the supernal Adamic sex creatures of permanent residence on the system capitals. 45:6.3 (516.1)

Page 141 ~ The Melchizedek Sons conduct upward of thirty different educational centers on Jerusem. These training schools begin with the college of self-evaluation and end with the schools of Jerusem citizenship, wherein the Material Sons and Daughters join with the Melchizedeks and others in their supreme effort to qualify the mortal survivors for the assumption of the high responsibilities of representative government. The entire universe is organized and administered on the representative plan. Representative government is the divine ideal of self-government among nonperfect beings. 45:7.3 (517.5)

Page 142 ~ The vote cast at a Jerusem election by any one personality has a value ranging from one up to one thousand. Jerusem citizens are thus classified in accordance with their mota achievement. 45:7.6 (518.2)

Page 145 ~ This Jerusem broadcast-receiving station is encircled by an enormous amphitheater, constructed of scintillating materials largely unknown on Urantia and seating over five billion beings — material and morontia — besides accommodating innumerable spirit personalities. It is the favorite diversion for all Jerusem to spend their leisure at the broadcast station, there to learn of the welfare and state of the universe. And this is the only planetary activity which is not slowed down during the recession of light. 46:3.2 (522.2)

Page 147 ~ These circular reservations of the Sons occupy an enormous area, and until nineteen hundred years ago there existed a great open space at its center. This central region is now occupied by the Michael memorial, completed some five hundred years ago. Four hundred and ninety-five years ago, when this temple was dedicated, Michael was present in person, and all Jerusem heard the touching story of the Master Son's bestowal on Urantia, the least of Satania. The Michael memorial is now the center of all activities embraced in the modified management of the system occasioned by Michael's bestowal, including most of the more recently transplanted Salvington activities. The memorial staff consists of over one million personalities. 46:5.19 (525.1)

Page 149 ~ On the fifth mansonia you begin to learn of the constellation study worlds. Here you meet the first of the instructors who begin to prepare you for the subsequent constellation sojourn. More of this preparation continues on worlds six and seven, while the finishing touches are supplied in the sector of the ascending mortals on Jerusem. 47:7.4 (537.4)

Page 149 ~ A real birth of cosmic consciousness takes place on mansonia number five. You are becoming universe minded. This is indeed a time of expanding horizons. It is beginning to dawn upon the enlarging minds of the ascending mortals that some stupendous and magnificent, some supernal and divine, destiny awaits all who complete the progressive Paradise ascension, which has been so laboriously but so joyfully and auspiciously begun. At about this point the average mortal ascender begins to manifest bona fide experiential enthusiasm for the Havona ascent. Study is becoming voluntary, unselfish service natural, and worship spontaneous. A real morontia character is budding; a real morontia creature is evolving. 47:7.5 (537.5)

Page 150 ~ The entire universe is one vast school. 37:6.2 (412.2)

Page 150 ~ The mortal-survival plan has a practical and serviceable objective; you are not the recipients of all this divine labor and painstaking training only that you may survive just to enjoy endless bliss and eternal ease. There is a goal of transcendent service concealed beyond the horizon of the present universe age. If the Gods designed merely to take you on one long and eternal joy excursion, they certainly would not so largely turn the whole universe into one vast and intricate practical training school, requisition a substantial part of the celestial creation as teachers and instructors, and then spend ages upon ages piloting you, one by one, through this gigantic universe school of experiential training. The furtherance of the scheme of mortal progression seems to be one of the chief businesses of the present organized universe, and the majority of innumerable orders of created intelligences are either directly or indirectly engaged in advancing some phase of this progressive perfection plan. 48:8.3 (558.1)

Page 152 ~ Sojourners on this sphere are permitted to visit transition world number six, where they learn more about the high spirits of the superuniverse, although they are not able to visualize many of these celestial beings. Here they also receive their first lessons in the prospective spirit career which so immediately follows graduation from the morontia training of the local universe. 47:8.1 (537.6)

Page 152 ~ The assistant System Sovereign makes frequent visits to this world, and the initial instruction is here begun in the technique of universe administration. The first lessons embracing the affairs of a whole universe are now imparted. 47:8.2 (537.7)

Page 152 ~ During the sojourn on world number six the mansion world students achieve a status which is comparable with the exalted development characterizing those evolutionary worlds which have normally progressed beyond the initial stage of light and life. The organization of society on this mansonia is of a high order. The shadow of the mortal nature grows less and less as these worlds are ascended one by one. You are becoming more and more adorable as you leave behind the coarse vestiges of planetary animal origin. 47:8.7 (538.5)

Page 153 ~ Coming up through great tribulation' serves to make glorified mortals very kind and understanding, very sympathetic and tolerant. 47:8.7 (538.5)

Page 155 ~ Before leaving the mansion worlds, all mortals will have permanent seraphic associates or guardians. And as you ascend the morontia spheres, eventually it is the seraphic guardians who witness and certify the decrees of your eternal union with the Thought Adjusters. Together they have established your personality identities as children of the flesh from the worlds of time. Then, with your attainment of the mature morontia estate, they accompany you through Jerusem and the associated worlds of system progress and culture. After that they go with you to Edentia and its seventy spheres of advanced socialization, and subsequently will they pilot you to the Melchizedeks and follow you through the superb career of the universe headquarters worlds. And when you have learned the wisdom and culture of the Melchizedeks, they will take you on to Salvington, where you will stand face to face with the Sovereign of all Nebadon. And still will these seraphic guides follow you through the minor and major sectors of the superuniverse and on to the receiving worlds of Uversa, remaining with you until you finally enseconaphim for the long Havona flight. 113:7.4 (1248.4)

Page 156 ~ The experience on this sphere is the crowning achievement of the immediate postmortal career. Any discernible differences between those mortals hailing from the isolated and retarded worlds and those survivors from the more advanced and enlightened spheres are virtually obliterated during the sojourn on the seventh mansion world. Here you will be purged of all the remnants of unfortunate heredity, unwholesome environment, and unspiritual planetary tendencies. The last remnants of the "mark of the beast" are here eradicated. 47:9.1 (538.6)

Page 157 ~ While sojourning on mansonia number seven, permission is granted to visit transition world number seven, the world of the Universal Father. Here you begin a new and more spiritual worship of the unseen Father, a habit you will increasingly pursue all the way up through your long ascending career. 47:9.2 (538.7)

Page 167 ~ Mighty Messengers, in common with all Trinity-embraced sons, are assigned to all phases of superuniverse activities. They maintain constant connection with their headquarters through the superuniverse reflectivity service. Mighty Messengers serve in all sectors of a superuniverse and frequently execute missions to the local universes and even to the individual worlds. 22:2.7 (245.7)

Page 168 ~ The sending of Adjusters, their indwelling, is indeed one of the unfathomable mysteries of God the Father. These fragments of the divine nature of the Universal Father carry with them the potential of creature immortality. Adjusters are immortal spirits, and union with them confers eternal life upon the soul of the fused mortal. 40:7.1 (448.8)

Page 168 ~ These indwelling fragments of God are with your order of being from the early days of physical existence through all of the ascending career in Nebadon and Orvonton and on through Havona, even to Paradise itself. Thereafter, in the eternal adventure, this same Adjuster is one with you and of you. 40:7.3 (449.1)

Page 168 ~ The spirits of mortal fusion always ascend to the level of origin; such spirit entities unfailingly return to the sphere of primal source. 40:10.1 (452.1)

Page 168 ~ The Thought Adjuster, hailing from the Father on Paradise, never stops until the mortal son stands face to face with the eternal God. 40:10.2 (452.2)

Page 168 ~ Adjuster-fused ascenders do indeed have a grand and glorious career as finaliters spread out before them in the eternal future. Adjuster-fused mortals are destined to penetrate the universe of universes. 40:10.5 (452.5)

Page 168 ~ When the evolving soul and the divine Adjuster are finally and eternally fused, each gains all of the experiencible qualities of the other. This co-ordinate personality possesses all of the experiential memory of survival once held by the ancestral mortal mind and then resident in the morontia soul, and in addition thereto this potential finaliter embraces all the experiential memory of the Adjuster throughout the mortal indwellings of all time. But it will require an eternity of the future for an Adjuster ever completely to endow the personality partnership with the meanings and values which the divine Monitor carries forward from the eternity of the past. 110:7.5 (1212.6)

Page 168 ~ Thought Adjuster fusion imparts eternal actualities to personality which were previously only potential. Among these new endowments may be mentioned: fixation of divinity quality, past -eternity experience and memory, immortality, and a phase of qualified potential absoluteness. 112:7.1 (1237.3)

Page 169 ~ When fusion with the Adjuster has been effected, there can be no future danger to the eternal career of such a personality. 112:7.4 (1237.6)

Page 169 ~ When the self attains the spiritual level, it has become a secure value in the universe, and this new value is predicated upon the fact that survival decisions have been made, which fact has been witnessed by eternal fusion with the Thought Adjuster. 112:7.6 (1238.1)

Page 169 ~ This extraordinary partnership is one of the most engrossing and amazing of all the cosmic phenomena of this universe age. 112:7.11 (1238.6)

Page 169 ~ With Adjuster fusion the Universal Father has completed his promise of the gift of himself to his material creatures; he has fulfilled the promise, and consummated the plan, of the eternal bestowal of divinity upon humanity. Now begins the human attempt to realize and to actualize the limitless possibilities that are inherent in the supernal partnership with God which has thus factualized. 112:7.14 (1239.3)

Page 169 ~ The present known destiny of surviving mortals is the Paradise Corps of the Finality; this is also the goal of destiny for all Thought Adjusters who become joined in eternal union with their mortal companions. At present the Paradise finaliters are working throughout the grand universe in many undertakings, but we all conjecture that they will have other and even more supernal tasks to perform in the distant future after the seven superuniverses have become settled in light and life, and when the finite God has finally emerged from the mystery which now surrounds this Supreme Deity. 112:7.15 (1239.4)

Page 169 ~ What an adventure! What a romance! A gigantic creation to be administered by the children of the Supreme, these personalized and humanized Adjusters, these Adjusterized and eternalized mortals, these mysterious combinations and eternal associations of the highest known manifestation of the essence of the First Source and Center and the lowest form of intelligent life capable of comprehending and attaining the Universal Father. 112:7.18 (1239.7)

Page 171 ~ ...what a beautiful occasion when mortals thus forgather to witness the ascension of their loved ones in spiritual flames, and what a contrast to those earlier ages when mortals must commit their dead to the embrace of the terrestrial elements! The scenes of weeping and wailing characteristic of earlier epochs of human evolution are now replaced by ecstatic joy and the most sublime enthusiasm... 55:2.5 (623.5)

Made in the USA
Middletown, DE
14 July 2018